Somebody's Business

Nickel Hill
Book Three

Irene Bennett Brown

Somebody's Business
Paperback Edition
Copyright © 2023 (As Revised) Irene Bennett Brown

Wolfpack Publishing
9850 S. Maryland Parkway, Suite A-5 #323
Las Vegas, Nevada 89183

wolfpackpublishing.com

Paperback ISBN 978-1-63977-782-2
eBook ISBN 978-1-63977-783-9

*To my faithful readers everywhere
and to my most helpful husband, Bob*

SOMEBODY'S BUSINESS

ONE

Despite the gurgling of the flooded, runaway creek in back of the house, it was a beautiful day. Sunshine warmed the cool air and white clouds fluffed in the blue sky. Jocelyn Pladson hastened toward the house with a basket of eggs from the henhouse, her small son, Andy, trotting along at her skirts. She did her best to shake off sadness at thought of the horrible flooding in so much of Kansas this spring, taking lives, destroying homes and businesses. Washing away roads and farmland. Kansas folks would long remember this year nineteen-six, but could be glad it wasn't so bad as that San Francisco earthquake in April. She'd seen the horror of that in the picture slides on her neighbor, Mabel Goody's stereoscope and she'd never forget it.

There was talk among neighbors that most of Kansas's flooding troubles were tapering off which meant they could set about normal life, take up travel again. Clearly, their creek wasn't quite so full and rampant. First thing, she'd make a trip to town for her talk with her friend Edna Ann Lockhart. Edna was desperate to sell the Skiddy Livery Stable, her husband, Carl, having died so sudden from typhoid that turned into pneumonia. Gone from Edna's life, gone from running the business. Edna Ann had implored Jocelyn to please buy the whole affair, the livery barn, pens and pastures. Jocelyn could get back into the business of buying and selling mules, which she'd been pretty good at in the past, working with her boss, Whit Hanley. Edna Ann would have the money from the sale to join the only family she had left, in Louisiana. She'd start over there.

Jocelyn grimaced and rubbed her cheek with her free hand, her steps slowing. It was ridiculous for her to own a business. A dress shop or restaurant, maybe. But a livery stable—a woman hostler? Not to mention the absence of money to buy? She stopped in her tracks, thinking.

"What's the matter, Momma?" Andy asked, his face puckered. He waited.

"Nothing's the matter, hon, Momma was just thinking."

"You make funny faces when you're thinkin'."

She laughed and kept going. "Yes, I suppose I do."

Her mind picked up where it left off as she opened the back door and Andy scuttled into the kitchen ahead of her. She couldn't help being excited, thinking of what owning her own business would be like. Money from the livery and mule sales, if she were running matters profitably—and she would put her shoulder to that end—could help in many ways at Nickel Hill Ranch.

A decision had to be made one way or the other,

and soon. Best to keep in mind that she already had endless responsibilities with family here on the ranch, and stop dreaming.

She settled Andy happily at play in the front room with the cardboard barn and carved wood animals she and Pete had made for him. She knelt beside him, ruffled his sandy-colored hair and gave the top of his head a kiss, smiling when he crowed for the toy red rooster in his hand, then sent it chasing after a clucking hen. Pretty clever observation for a three-year-old going on four, she thought, puffed with pride. He was a little farm boy, after all.

Moving about her small kitchen, she stored the eggs in the icebox, taking a second to admire the vanilla custard pudding she'd made for supper before she closed the door to the icebox. She sorted beans and put them to soak for supper on the back of the stove, the teakettle to the front for a cup of tea, her mind as busy as her hands. Wishing now that she hadn't taken Carl, Edna Ann's husband, so much for granted the many times she and Pete had used his services at the livery. He'd died so unexpectedly, leaving Edna Ann alone, to grieve and face a mountain of problems.

A few days after Carl Lockhart's funeral, Edna Ann confided to Jocelyn that her only family left was a much younger sister she'd never met. "She lives in Louisiana with her husband and she's expecting a baby. We've written letters back and forth for years and now she wants me to come. I'd like to meet her, help with her baby." Grasping Jocelyn's hand and wiping her eyes with the handkerchief in her other hand, she'd added, "To make it happen, I *have to sell* the livery. I'll need the money for such a trip, and to start a new life."

Jocelyn's heart ached for her friend practically every day since.

An old friend of Carl's, a broken-down elderly cowboy, named Prank Morgan, had come to the funeral and stayed to help out by running the livery. He wasn't able to buy the business, but he was willing to stay on and work for the person who bought it. "I'm desperate," Edna added, ending the conversation. "Couldn't you buy it, Jocelyn, please?"

Sitting at the table and blowing at her hot cup of tea, Jocelyn considered that this could be a perfect opportunity to get back into the mule trading business as well as owning the livery. There'd been problems in the past, but she'd enjoyed much of her time with mule herding and selling. Her efforts were profitable for her boss, she'd earned well from the project, too.

Such income now would be blessed welcome. Help to finance needed improvements here at the ranch. Like building on a summer kitchen, which she'd long wanted. They could make repairs to their worn-out old wagon, and to their buckboard. Maybe invest in a fine new buggy and team? Blamed if she wouldn't love new parlor tables and a piano, too.

In her mind's eye as she sipped her tea, she viewed the livery operation in detail—the large barn and pens in back of the livery. There was good pasture but she'd need more graze to hold mules she'd buy and want to fatten up between sales. There was more pasturage close-by that could be rented or traded for, she felt sure. Critter as pasture rental payment. Livery services would continue, they'd stable travelers' horses. Offer buggy, wagon, and horse rental as always. Might have some hay, grain, and corn hauled in from the home place for the livery animals, to add to whatever else might be needed from George Jacobsen's Feed and Seed Store, down the way from the livery. She set her cup down, smiling to herself.

She suddenly realized that Andy's noisy play in the other room, seemingly his wooden pig having a grunting argument with the crowing rooster, had ended. How long had he been quiet? She pushed up from the table, started to call out to him, then stopped. Her beloved little boy had likely fallen asleep there on the floor, it wouldn't be the first time. He was still young enough to be prone to both a morning and afternoon nap. She moved quietly to the other room, saw the scattered toys, but no sign of Andy.

She hurried upstairs to the two bedrooms to see if he'd crawled onto a bed there, or was after a toy he'd left there. No sign of him. "Andy? Andy, where are you? If you're hiding, come out now to Momma—so I know where you are." Her breath caught in her chest when she waited and no response. Rushing back downstairs, she tripped on the next to bottom step and nearly fell. Hurrying to the screened back porch, she looked out into the yard toward the creek and her heart froze. He was almost to the flooded banks, a small wooden boat in his hand.

Flinging the screen door open and moving quickly down the steps she called out as quietly but firm as she could, "Andy, wait for me. Come back to Momma now." The soft churning sound of the creek gripped her heart as she made her way toward him.

He looked at her over his shoulder, then took another few confident steps toward the tumbling creek. Jocelyn moved fast, trembling head to foot, sweating, but calling as calmly as possible, "I have a cookie for you, sweetie."

Andy hesitated then turned, his small face screwed up with question. "A cookie? With raisins?" He scrambled in a run back toward her and she rushed forward and scooped him up into her arms, held him tight. The creek was a roiling horror over his little shoulder. What if she hadn't seen her beloved baby in time? Her legs weak, her heart thundering, she stumbled back to the house.

Trembling all over, she placed Andy on a chair at the kitchen table. With a shaking hand she poured a cup of milk, brought him two raisin speckled cookies. Carefully, she removed the boat from his small hand and rammed it into her apron pocket. Unable to stand on her feet a minute longer, she took another chair, eyes on her precious child who meant more to her than life itself. Trying to hide her tears, she wiped her face with her apron. He looked at her with worry, and she smiled.

She explained, not for the first time, "You mustn't go to the crick without an older person with you, Andy, remember?"

"I'm big." He puffed his chest out to prove it, looked up at her wide-eyed.

"No, you aren't, you're just a little boy, and nobody should go near the crick when it's flooding like it is now. Nobody. It's very dangerous, Son, no matter how big a person might be. I want you to promise me you'll stay away from the crick. I want you to always play in a safe place, the front porch or front yard, or in the house with Momma, so that nothing bad happens to you." She drew him to her chest. "Do you understand?"

"When I'm big as Rommy can I go to the crick?"

Jocelyn sighed. "When the crick is normal, not deep and flooding like it is now, and you're as big as your brother, Rommy, I think that'd be fine." Rommy, the young boy she and Pete had taken in and given a home to almost four years ago, was close to seventeen years old now. Six feet tall, lanky, a good-natured, likable young man. His childhood name, Rommy, was now more often than not shortened to Rom.

His father, Chester Treyhern, a widower and suspected cattle thief on the run, hadn't wanted to give Jocelyn and Pete legal custody of Rommy, as they wanted, but was perfectly willing for them to keep him as part of their family. Rommy was more than happy with the situation and after a year of referring to Jocelyn as ma'am, he now called her simply, 'Ma'. Pete was still Pete.

Andy, his eyelids drooping sleepily, asked, "Where's Rom? I want to tell him the crick is bad and I can't go there. Where's Papa? I want to tell him."

"They're searching the pastures for new baby calves. Helping the Mama cows if they need to. They'll be bringing the mama cows and their little calves to the barnyard pens tonight and we can go up to see them. Help some of the baby calves learn to suck milk from a bottle if they need us."

"Okay," he said sleepily. "Nila will go with us, too, to see the new baby calves?"

"I think she'll want to, yes, when she gets home from teaching school, and we've all had our supper." Nila, a distant cousin of hers, was another homeless young person they'd taken to live with them, like family, when the girl was fifteen going on sixteen. Her mother, Flaudie Malone, living in Missouri, had ignored their request to adopt Nila legally, had given no opinion one way or the other. Over time, Nila had gone from calling Jocelyn 'Mrs. Pladson' to most times, 'Jocelyn' and occasionally 'Ma'. Jocelyn gave a deep, satisfying sigh. *Hardly matters anymore, we couldn't love both Nila and Rom more if they were our born children.*

Nila was close to twenty years old now, just finishing her second-year teaching Gorham School. Three or four days a week in the summer, she waited tables in the hotel dining room in Skiddy. The young woman had wonderful dreams, and would likely fulfill them. Half of every dollar she earned, she saved for the traveling she wanted to do, as a journalist someday, sending back stories for newspapers. When she had any free time, her nose was in a book, studying.

Andy was about to fall from his chair, a raisin on his lip, half a cookie crumbled in his lap, his eyes closed. Jocelyn lifted him gently and carried his warm, limp little body upstairs to his small bed in her and Pete's room. She tucked him in for a nap with his sock monkey.

She looked down at him with her heart in her throat. He could have drowned today so easily in that awful creek, her precious child lost to her forever. It couldn't happen. He must grow up, tall and strong like his older brother, Rom, his daddy, Pete. She had to keep a close eye on him, all the time. How could she do that? Why was she even thinking for a minute that she could operate a business with all she had to do at home? Taking care of her family that was so dear to her?

On Saturday, Rom, dusty and sweaty from work in the barn, brought Jocelyn's mule team and wagon down to the house for her drive to Skiddy. She shooed her foraging chickens, noisily clucking, from the yard and toward the hen house and turned to him. "Thanks, Rom. Nila or I was going to hitch up these mules but glad you went ahead and did it for us."

She took a moment for her old mule friends, Alice and Zenith. She'd been through a lot with these beloved old mules and they meant the world to her. As she gave Alice a pat, Zenith brayed like a rusty gate opening. Jocelyn gave him a last stroke and turned with a laugh to climb into the wagon.

Rom touched his hat to her. "Ain't no trouble hitching these mules. I had to come out here to the well and drink me about a gallon of water anyways."

"Fine then. We'll be back by suppertime. Take a rest in the shade if you need to, Rom." He shrugged and headed off toward the well. She called after him, "There's fresh ginger cookies in the house, get yourself a handful."

"Splash plenty of that water on yourself, Rom," Nila called back over her shoulder, teasing.

As they set off, Jocelyn was thinking how much she loved this country, how glad she was that she and Gram had moved here to the Flint Hills from Kansas City years ago. On either side of the road, rolling tall-grass prairie spread as far as the eye could see. Pastures were speckled occasionally with grazing cattle, some long-horned, or wild horses running free. From time to time, a small cluster of ranch buildings showed in the distance. Above it all, an immense blue sky held beautiful cloud arrangements to entertain the eye.

She turned to smile at Nila, on the far side of their wagon seat, and down at Andy tucked between them. For most of the first mile, the young woman and little boy carried on a friendly argument about Andy's sock monkey. Did he come from darkest Africa, as Nila claimed, or Andy's bed as he insisted? "He's not from Aferka!" Andy shouted and doubled up laughing.

"Don't be too sure," Nila said with faked serious-ness. "I have a book from school that I'll show you. There are pictures of monkeys climbing trees in Africa and they look exactly like your monkey."

Andy shook his head and said quietly, "But he's not from Aferka. I know he's not."

"Yes," Nila answered, giving him a hug. "You're probably right, Andy. My mistake."

Jocelyn reflected on the time a few years back when Nila had been sent to live with them. A grave, anxious young girl, plain looking but not unattractive with straw blond hair worn in a coronet of braids. Bright, hazel eyes. Nila's guilt that her mother had forced her on the Pladsons soon vanished. She enjoyed where she was, worked hard, and in short order became a true member of the family. The time was coming, though, that Nila, full-grown now, would strike out on her own, fulfilling that dream to be a traveling journalist, writing about faraway places that most folks would never have a chance to see. *A fine young person,* Jocelyn thought, looking again at Nila and smiling to herself.

Pulling her thoughts away to what lay ahead, Jocelyn squared her shoulders and took a deep breath. She'd leave Nila and her small satchel off at the hotel.

So far, Nila enjoyed her off and on summer job waiting tables in the hotel's dining room, spending nights when necessary with another waitress in a small room off the hotel kitchen. That done, she'd continue on to the other end of town to give Edna Ann her decision. Let the poor woman down as gently as she could. It wasn't going to be easy, and she dreaded this more than anything else she could think of.

TWO

Jocelyn drove up to the tiny house, once painted bright green now faded to the color of summer's dying grass, set the brake and tied her team to the hitchrail outside the picket fence. Taking Andy's hand, and swallowing hard, she knocked at the front door. The heaviness of her heart was not helped by the happy, hopeful smile on Edna Ann's face as she opened the door.

"Come in, Jocelyn, dear, so glad you've come."

"Andy and I are happy to see you, too," Jocelyn spoke through a dry throat, finding it hard to smile naturally as they entered the front parlor.

Edna Ann gave her a hug and then turned to the boy. "Andy, I have three new kittens." She clapped her hands. "Would you like to see them?"

"Yup!" He nodded and trotted after Edna Ann as she led to the kitchen where the kittens lapped at a dish of milk.

Biting her lip, Jocelyn followed, wishing that she could do anything other than turn Edna Ann down.

With Andy happily playing with the kittens, the two women returned to the front room with cups of tea from the kitchen. "I'm sorry, Edna Ann." Jocelyn settled in a chair, had to get the worst behind them so that they could reason another answer for her friend. "I won't be buying the livery stable."

Edna Ann's eyes widened in surprise, she leaned forward, her hand going to her chest. Her face paled.

Jocelyn took a deep breath and added in a choked voice, "I've come to see that there's no way I can run a business proper, and not neglect my family—and I can't do that. I can't make them second in my life."

In another moment, Edna Ann's eyes glistened with tears of disappointment, worry. She sat still as stone as Jocelyn told her about the incident with Andy at the creek. "I'm so sorry, Edna Ann, I'd love to have the business, and more than anything I want to help you out of this predicament. Maybe, if we put our heads together, we can come up with another, better plan."

Shaking her head, Edna Ann put her tea aside, took a handkerchief from where it had been tucked in her sleeve and wiped her eyes. She spoke in a hollow voice, "You can't imagine what I'm up against, Jocelyn. I was so hoping you'd buy the livery, save it from being torn down, done away with."

"Done away with? Torn down? I don't understand." Jocelyn frowned in puzzlement. "It'd stay in operation, with a new owner the only change."

"I'm not just disappointed, Jocelyn, I'm scared to death what's about to happen in Skiddy if I can't find a buyer for the livery."

Jocelyn sat back, then forward and gulped her tea. She nodded for her to continue.

"It's that new hat shop owner, Maretta Rudd. She hates the livery stable, complains that when the wind blows, which I admit is most of the time, the smells coming from the livery are unbearable to her and her customers. I admit she's right about the smells, but there she is, setting up shop just two doors down. Why'd she do that if she wanted to be away from livery smells?"

"I can't imagine." Jocelyn bit her lip, and put her tea aside, her stomach churning.

"The fool woman rants on and on about what she calls 'riff raff'. The hardworking cowboys, ranchers, farmers, and others who just natural have business at the livery. She's spreading talk about town that instead of a buyer, it is a good time to be *rid of the livery for good.*"

"But that's darn fool nonsense. The town can't do without the services of a livery stable. It is a rancher or traveler's place to leave their horse, or team and wagon, when in town for any time. Not to mention the need of town-folk to rent a mount, or buggy and team. What on earth is the woman thinking?"

"It's her motorcar that she putts around in—"

"Motorcar?"

"Yes, motorcar, with her nose in the air, thinking she's better than anyone else, that's the problem. A scarlet red Ford Model A it is. No matter her fancy-dancy auto is one of a scarce few in hundreds of miles, she claims that autocars are coming into fashion quickly and 'the near dead town of Skiddy needs to get busy and accept progress'. Make a place for motorcars."

"That's balderdash." Jocelyn's concern fired up into anger. "There are few businesses as necessary as a livery stable, *right now.* Any change over to motorcars as transportation is likely years in the future and will be gradual, not overnight like she's saying. Skiddy is not ready. She's blind, thinking anything else." *Or a pure idiot.*

"As you probably know, there's one other owner of a motorcar in town and Maretta has him, J.L. Cochran, siding with her, and she with him. You know the one who bought out the ice and coal business, and the lumber and hardware store?"

"I know a little about Jessop Cochran. A jolly sort, fine clothes, new in town and friendly as all get-out. I understand that he dabbles in land buying and selling, too. Not just businesses here in Skiddy."

"Yes, to all that, and the way he acts a body would think he wants to own the town, make Skiddy his own little kingdom, Miss Rudd his queen. The man is plaguing me to sell out to him for a price so low it's next to nothing." She chewed her bottom lip and her eyes darkened. "He says the price is right because he only wants the land, not the business, which he has no use for. He'd be tearing down the livery."

Jocelyn sagged back in her chair, near speechless, a cold knot beginning to form inside her. If Mr. Cochran and Miss Rudd carried through with such a thoughtless, ignorant plan, it would leave Edna Ann destitute. Mr. Morgan, who worked for Edna Ann, would be without a livelihood, a place to go. An entire part of the country, not just the town, would be left without the necessities of a central livery stable. "Surely this cock and bull plan will blow over?" Her heart overflowed with sympathy for Edna Ann. Joined by unmitigated anger and twinges of fear toward the pair opposing her friend. Could they actually do this?

"I wish I could count on their failing at their intentions." Edna Ann's face was drawn with worry as she spoke. "From what I've heard, Mr. Cochran's foot was stepped on by a horse when he was a child, mangling it, an' he's always hated horses, wanted nothing to do with them personally. His means of transportation has been trolleys in the city, stagecoach and trains. Thinks mules are disgusting. A motorcar is the thing, with him, and he preaches it loud and long all over town. Miss Rudd, Maretta, is after as many women in town as possible to agree with her, that the livery needs to go, because of the smells and all. Some, not friends of mine, agree. Claiming it is about time, that she's right."

"Well, she isn't!" There was an edge to her laugh. "The livery is needed, and will continue to be for a good long time yet. Maretta Rudd is a fool and should keep her mind on making and selling her fancy hats. And you're right, why did she set up business so close to the livery? Doesn't she know that little building she's in used to be a saddlery and bootmaker's shop? Old odors of cow-hide and tanning oils from her own establishment could be what's bothering her, not all the cause of the livery."

"I—I hope most of folks around here feel as you and I do, Jocelyn." Looking desperate for support, Edna Ann swallowed. "And put down this woman's idea right away. I have to find me somebody to sell the business to as it is, somebody who'll keep it in operation. George down at the feed store likes the idea of your taking over the livery, if nobody else does."

"George has been a good friend to Pete and me from the time we took over Nickel Hill Ranch, and the feed store in some ways is a companion business to the livery."

"You would've been perfect, Jocelyn, but I understand that you have to put your family first, and you have all that work to do at the ranch, too."

Jocelyn's jaw clamped. *I sure do, cooking, cleaning, canning, feeding chickens and the pigs, milking the cow, weeding the garden, doing the wash, seeing to my family's needs—it's all endless.*

They had moved into the kitchen to check on Andy, who was still fascinated by the furry little kittens. Edna Ann got down on her knees and began to tell Andy the name of each kitten. "This yellow one, I call Fluffy. The black one is—Blacky. Dusty is the name I gave the little grey kitty." The look on the woman's face, and on Andy's was priceless as they took turns cuddling the kittens floundering about in a large basket.

Jocelyn felt horrible, turning Edna Ann down. She looked on, remembering that Carl and Edna Ann had never been able to have children of their own. It would be so good for Edna Ann to live with her sister and help with the baby, watching the child grow up. She was the aunt to the child, after all.

She had to do something to help her dear friend make the move she was dreaming of, and keep the livery for the town at the same time. There had to be a way. The Skiddy Livery Stable had been there in the same spot near the far end of town since the community was founded in 1870 and the town named after a railroad tycoon, Francis Skiddy. The livery was not going anywhere!

Jocelyn told Edna Ann goodbye and to not give up hope, they'd figure out something, because neither Miss

Maretta Rudd or J.L. Cochran had the brains of a goose. They were completely wrong in what they wanted to do and needed to be convinced of that in short order.

Telling herself that she wanted a quick look-see and that was all, Jocelyn, with Andy beside her, drove her wagon another few blocks to the livery stable. It was her first opportunity to meet the old wrangler that Edna Ann had hired and as she climbed from the wagon and helped Andy down, she studied him, a short bow-legged figure, coming toward her from the shadows of the livery barn. His features were coarse, leathery, wrinkled. Battered ears poked out of his bristly whitish-sandy hair; his bushy eyebrows and moustache matched his hair. His grey eyes above his broad crooked nose were lively and kind and he wore a wide, welcoming grin. "H'lo, ma'am. Can I do somehin' for ya?"

"Nice to meet you, Mr. Morgan, I'm Mrs. Pladson. This is my little boy, Andy." She adjusted Andy on her hip and took the old man's gnarled, calloused hand when he offered it. "If you don't mind, I'd like to take a close look around the stables, the hay barn, and outside."

"Don't mind a'tall," he said with a wide grin, leading the way. "You're the friend of Missus Lockhart that's lookin' to buy this outfit?"

"I'm Mrs. Pladson, yes. Jocelyn Pladson, but I'm afraid I won't be buying the livery. I just want to take a walk about the property, try and think of some way to help Edna Ann."

He stopped to tell her, his brow furrowed, "I sure wanted to help out when I heard Carl was sick. He saved my life, ya know, when we was a'fightin' that war with the cussed South. It was in the Battle of Wilson

Creek that I took a Minnie ball to the belly. Me and Carl Lockhart was Missouri boys, grew up together. He damned sure wasn't goin' to let me die. A young woman from Kansas, visitin' friends who lived not too far on horseback from the battlefield, was where Carl took me. She was one fine nurse, that little gal, Edna Ann. Her and Carl became man and wife soon as the war was over."

"That's a wonderful story, Mr. Morgan, how the two of them, Edna Ann and Carl, saved you." Andy slid down from her arms to look at a caterpillar on a dandelion growing close to the barn door. He jumped up to follow when she and Morgan entered the livery stable. Four horse stalls were occupied, Jocelyn saw through the rails, a black lying down, a blue roan, tossing his head, pacing and whickering, and two sorrels seeming to observe the humans. She smiled, had always liked the horse and hay smells of a barn, the soft sounds of horses munching feed, blowing, huffing, and stomping. The sweet smell of milk and baby calves when it was a cow barn. This horse barn was decently clean, nearby was a wheelbarrow of dung that Mr. Morgan had been scooping up.

"Well, yes, 'tis," he said of the Lockhart couple saving his life. "I'm glad to be here where I'm needed. Durn sorry I can't buy the place my ownself from Edna Ann. Sure wish it was you buyin' it and not that Cockroach fella that keeps botherin' her."

"J.L. Cochran, the man who bought the hardware store?" Her heart thudded heavily in her chest.

"Yep. Cochran the Cockroach. Him or that lady friend of his, the hat lady, ain't worth shootin', either one, the things they think's gotta be done in a damn big rush, to this pretty little town." He reddened. "S'cuse my language."

Jocelyn nodded, her manner firm. "I tend to agree, Mr. Morgan. They have to be stopped."

"A bullet for him and one for her would do it, like back in the war 'tween the states, but they's laws against that."

"Bang!" Andy pointed a stick he'd been playing with into the air. "Bang!" He looked up at them and grinned with pride.

"No," Jocelyn frowned at the same time she fought not to laugh. "No bullets. We'll be nice about it, but we will change their minds, scotch their plans or else. Right, Mr. Morgan?"

"Well, sure you're karec. I just wish you was buyin' the place, that would take care of everythin' all t'once. I'd sure work hard for you, ma'am, if you did. And I wish you'd call me Prank, like everybody else does."

She turned to look at him from where she was petting the neck of a pretty sorrel mare over its stall gate. "Prank? That's your name?" Her smile wavered as she waited.

He explained, "I warn't the pretty baby my ma was countin' on when I was born, ya' see. Looked like a toad. Yup, ugly little toad, ever'body said. Ma cried, I was tole, and she wondered 'why God would play such a prank on her, givin' her such a toady babe'."

Jocelyn's face screwed up in sympathy. She opened her mouth to say something kindly but he wasn't finished.

"My brother, two years older'n me, called me Prank a few times. Then Pa did, Ma did, too, and the name stuck."

"That doesn't seem fair, or right to me." *Why couldn't they give him a regular little boy's name and use that?*

"The name don't bother me none, missus. Reckon I'm glad they didn't name me 'Toad'. I made me use of my name 'Prank' when I was a young'un. Had me good times playin' jokes, bein' a *pranker* 'an makin' folks laugh. One time I switched salt into the sugar bowl and ruined Ma and Pa's cups of coffee. Got switched good for that, though." He laughed at himself. "Made big snowballs with horse-apple dung in the center to throw from hidin' at folks walkin' along the street." He sighed, and looked off into the distance. "Playin' jokes on folks stopped when I got taken on as a soldier. Too young even for whiskers, I fought for the Union at Wilson Creek an' I'm mighty proud'a that. Growed up fast." He looked at her. "Yeh, Missus Pladson, don't worry none about me, I like my name."

He showed her the livery's office, hardly more than a cubbyhole. There was a small window that faced the street, fortunately, *or maybe not fortunately*, she thought. The space contained a beat-up desk holding a lamp, and two chairs. In another section of the room, behind a canvas curtain, was a cot with an old trunk at the foot of it and a side table holding a lamp. A barn coat hung from a nail in the wall. Prank's quarters smelled of sweat and tobacco.

They continued the tour outside, checking two large fenced fields of bluestem grass where two more horses, a dark bay gelding and a sorrel mare grazed. Circled through the holding pens, the wood feed and water troughs. Jocelyn hesitated below the tinny clank and whir of the windmill to look it all over a second time. *What woman in her right mind would want to own a livery stable?* Her mind chased the thought for a moment and she knew for certain. *I do, I want this.* She resisted the urge to spin in a wild circle, pressed her lips tight to keep from smiling like an idiot.

Minutes later, they entered the large cavernous hay barn that also contained rental wagons and buggies, and a large tack room filled with neatly arranged saddles, halters, bridles, stirrups, ropes, horse blankets and more. Nothing fancy but all clean and most in good repair. *A setup just right for buying and selling mules as well as livery service.* They continued the tour in quiet, Jocelyn's thoughts torn with what she'd do if the place were hers. But it couldn't be. *Or could it?*

Prank broke the silence. "That cockroach is a fool, thinkin' a fancy buildin' sellin' them horseless carriage contraptions should be put on Carl and Edna's property. Just because him and the hat woman got them, and think they's grand, don't mean other folks can go off and buy their ownselves a la-de-dah motorcar. Hardly nobody can afford 'em, you kin' near buy a small farm with that amount of money. Mostly, the bigheaded fool just wants to run things, his an' her way a'course, whether it makes good sense or not."

I'm afraid you have that exactly right, Mr. Morgan— um, Prank.

He paced, his brow wrinkling. "A man was here the other day, who told me J.L. Cockroach was about to be tarred and feathered if he didn't leave Eskridge, the last town he done business in. They'd had enough of his cheatin' and 'take over' greed. Fella was givin' me a warnin' is what he was doin'. I don't have me the full details, but if I ever get 'em, I'll use 'em against him an' he won't see another day in Skiddy, Kansas after that!"

Jocelyn nodded without answering.

After trailing back into the stable, Andy's hand in hers. it was time to go.

She touched the hostler's arm, "Thank you for this afternoon, Mr.—uh, Prank. I've liked our talk and it has given me some ideas." For one thing, she'd like to learn more of what he'd just told her about Mr. Cochran. J.L. Cochran hadn't been in Skiddy long enough for folks to really know him, as likable and kind as he seemed to be at first. Clearly, there was more to him than that and it was important that they have a look into his past, what all he was up to in Skiddy.

On the way home to the ranch, Andy asleep on the wagon seat with his head in her lap, her hand on his small shoulder, her other hand holding the reins, Jocelyn gave Alice and Zenith their head and allowed her thoughts full sweep.

Returning to tell Edna Ann goodbye today, she'd all but promised that she'd find a way to take over the livery business. Not a guarantee that she would, but leaning that way. Somebody with good sense had to, and quick. Maretta and J.L. must have conveniently put from mind that there were few machines to take over the work of horses and mules. Mules were dependable and smart, often more so than horses—with plowing, drawing heavy dray loads, and grading roads. In the city they drew trolleys and delivery wagons. The need for intelligent mules and yes, horse power, too, was endless and would be for years to come.

Most everyone traveled horseback, or drove a buggy or wagon behind a team of horses or mules. Transportation they could afford and were satisfied with as far as she could tell. The discussions she'd heard among friends about motorcars were *complaints* about the noisy things scaring their animals. The time might come when a motorcar would be an actual need for most folks. For now, the livery stable, the work of horses and mules, held a strong foothold in every part of the universe, not just in Skiddy, Kansas. Change might come, but not yet.

THREE

"Pete, I love you, love my family more than anything else on earth." Jocelyn fought tears as the two of them sat for a brief talk at the kitchen table after supper, the kerosene lamp spilling a light on their faces. "I didn't want to worry you the other day, when you came in so late and tired from the barn. I meant to tell you, more than once, how close Andy came to falling in the creek, to being swept away from us forever in that terrible water." She wiped her eyes, tried to sip her cooling coffee and couldn't swallow. She put the cup down. "I was ashamed, to tell the truth, for not keeping a better eye on our little one. That will never, ever, happen again."

"It's all right, sweetheart. You found him in time, kept him from falling in." His work roughened hand caught hers and his expression warmed with affection. "Honey, there's no better Momma on earth than you. Nila and Rom have a good home they didn't have before they came to us. They're happy contented young folks because of you." He thumbed toward the living

room where Nila's jubilant voice was reading aloud to
Andy as if she were the talking animals, making Andy
bubble with loud laughter.

"You're right, Pete, those two are having a good
time." Jocelyn rubbed her arm, smiled in satisfaction.
"Rom does, too, spending hours, when he can, training
that mule, Shay, to do tricks. For the sake of Hannah,
what's next? That young man has taught that mule to
smile, to jump a fence, to stand on a stump and bray like
he's preaching. All of it by telling that mule how
wonderful he is, and treating him with carrots from my
garden. Sometimes I wonder if I'll have any carrots
left." She smiled and reflected, "Carrots don't matter,
though. We have good youngsters like you say, and they
do matter."

"Darn right." Grinning, Pete pulled her to her feet,
and drew her into his arms. "You dote on that little son
of ours the clock around. You're a beautiful, loving wife
and mother. You've got no reason to harp on yourself
like you've been. If you'd like to get back into the mule
trading business, the Skiddy livery as headquarters, we
can make it happen. We'll figure it out, sweetheart."

"Do you really think so, Pete?" She looked up at
him. "I learned a lot about caring for mules, buying and
selling them, from my summer working for Whit
Hanley. Not to mention working with my mules on the
farm before I lost the property to the bank. Judging
mules for their best traits, their age, their worth—I could
do that part of it, I know." Her spirits soared, discussing
the matter, then leveled off, went flat. "But when it
comes to it, my real goal in this life is to see that my
family, each one of you, thrive—against all harm or
handicap."

He kissed her forehead, stroked her back. "I understand what you're saying. I feel the same towards you and the young'uns. You mean everything to me, Jocey. I couldn't take it if something bad happened to any of you."

"I suppose it's my own past that makes me so determined to do right by my family." She rubbed the side of her face, thinking. *It's the gospel truth and I darn well know it.* "Being bullied for how I looked, before I had surgery for my cleft mouth."

She stiffened her back and forced the trembling in her voice away as she continued, "Never getting to know my mother because she died when I was a baby. Then my school-teacher Pa took off, a drifter for years, grieving for my mother." Her shoulders lifted then lowered in a deep sigh. "Being raised by my sick Grandma Letty. Then, it was hardly a cinch for a twelve-year-old girl to take over and see to Gram's survival and my own. Pete," feeling an acute sense of purpose, she gave a nod. "I will see to it that nothing like that happens to my loved ones, or I'll die trying. But I practically promised Edna Ann, before I left her on Saturday, that I'd buy the livery, save her from her worry, her problems."

She felt Pete's thoughtful eyes on her as she retrieved the coffee pot from the stove and refilled their cups with fresh, hot coffee. Most of the time, she didn't fuss so much, but this was family they were talking about. She motioned them back to the table.

Pete's fingers furrowed his hair, he scraped back his chair and sat down. "You did the right thing, Jocey, making the promise, to help that poor widowed woman." He pulled the pitcher of cream toward him and poured a splash into his coffee. "You're one of the smartest, ablest women I know. Everybody we know feels that way about you, all you've been through, and the good you've made happen single-handed in your life. Like when you didn't realize you were having truck with outlaws until they abandoned you with a herd of mules. An' you took good care of the mules like you'd done it all your young life."

"Former outlaws," she corrected. "They were changed to better, good men. Serious troubles they had to deal with took them away, leaving me by myself."

He nodded, and continued, "I'm fine with your buying the Skiddy livery, running it and a mule trading business. Why else would Edna Ann Lockhart turn to you to take over now that Carl's gone, but that she knows you can do it? That you'd be happy in the doing. It's going to be somebody's business, why not yours?"

The incident with Andy and the flooded creek again filled her mind and Jocelyn felt sick. She insisted, "My family has to come first, Pete. I won't abandon you and the young ones, not for a business, not for anything."

"You won't have to abandon anybody," he argued with a half-smile, pouring coffee into his saucer and blowing on it to cool it. "We'll keep that ol' civil war veteran, Prank, on, to handle the day-to-day livery work. You can take Andy with you when you need to be at the business, maybe a day or two a week to see what's needed. Nila and Rom will help, like they've always done. Good workers. The livery stable can be a fine side business to Nickel Hill Ranch, an investment for our future, and our young'uns, too."

"I don't know, Pete, are you sure?" Her heart was

thumping hard in anticipation mixed with concern. Her saucer rattled when she put her cup down.

"Yep, I am. At the start we'll have to tighten our belts and struggle some moneywise." He spread his sun-browned hands. "But the mule business in the long run can be a money maker. Mules are the hardest workers when it comes to ranching and farming, always a need for them. There's ways to save." He leaned forward, setting his cup aside. "We can supplement the livery's pastures by raising hay, oats, corn, here on the ranch, to feed the stock we keep in town. The pulling teams for those whose only choice is to hire them. The mules you'll have on hand 'til they're prime and fit to sell. Along with the horses Prank puts up at the livery for the owners in town to do business."

"That sounds fine, Pete, and as much as I want to help Edna Ann, must help her, we don't have the ready money to march into town and buy her out. Not without borrowing from the bank and we agreed, Pete," she gave him a level look, "from the moment Nickel Hill became ours, that there'd never be bank loans to worry about, unless we hit positive bottom and we'd have no other choice."

He smiled at her. "This ain't the bottom, hon, it's the way up."

She hesitated for several noisy ticks of the wall clock. "I suppose." She smiled back at him, beginning to relax. "The price Edna Ann is asking is fair reasonable, to start with."

"We can sell off some cattle. If necessary, we can use some of the money we've been holding onto so's we could add more land to Nickel Hill. In time, when the business is solid and paying back, we can add more pasturage to the ranch, and replace any cattle we had to sell early."

Jocelyn weighed their conversation against her thoughts. "Nila and Rom are old enough to soon be on their own. I want to give them the best start that we can, in whatever they choose for their life's work. We owe them, Pete. They couldn't be more like our own children."

"We do owe them, true. I reckon Rom will want a horse farm or some such of his own by then." He wisecracked, scratching his jaw, "Providing we can get his mind off trick riding and roping and wanting to join up with Buffalo Bill's show, or follow Red Miller down to Oklahoma and be a cowboy performer in the 101 Ranch Real West Show."

They were both quiet a moment, thinking. Jocelyn spoke first, "That rascal, Red Miller, had to leave us high and dry after he heard about the Miller Brothers 101 Ranch Real West Show appearing in Coffeeville, Kansas last year." She flipped her hand in the air. "Having missed seeing them and thinking that he, his name being Miller, might be related—God forbid—he had to take himself down to Oklahoma where the huge Miller ranch is, and find out." She shook her head, looking at the floor and then back up at Pete. "That man's a quandary if there ever was one, from the time he hired on to help you here on the ranch. And before."

"Can't argue that." He grinned. Red Miller was his good friend and always would be.

She made a face. "Then we get that short letter from Red at Christmas. Telling that none of them down there knew for sure if he's related to their Miller clan or not but they were awful nice to him. He'd 'stay on a while, join the other performers in the Miller show, and see if he liked it'."

"Lordamighty, hon, what if that's what our boy, Rom, would want to do?"

Or be a saddle bum like Red, follow in his footsteps? "You never know. He spends a lot of time teaching his funny mule, Shay, tricks. Like Red used to show him how to do using one of his favorite horses. With all of that, I'm still pure glad I gave Shay to Rom for keeps, after his poor ugly horse, Handsome, died quietly of old age. He loves that mule so much." She laughed softly, sipping her coffee. "Rom doesn't call the mule 'Shay' much. Short for the name I gave him, Ricochet—for bouncing off this and that. 'Mule' or 'my Mule' is all the name he uses nowadays for that beautiful fourteen-hands-high mule colt."

Pete chuckled in agreement.

She continued, scooting her chair back to stand. "I suppose we can't stop our young ones from following their own dreams. I know for sure I don't want Nila to always be a poorly paid country school teacher and working summers at the hotel for pennies. For all she wants to do, she'll likely need some studying she hasn't had yet. College. Or maybe, if she's lucky, an apprenticeship with a newspaper or magazine that does that sort of thing."

Jocelyn took their cups to the dishpan and quickly washed and dried them and stowed them in the cupboard. She said over her shoulder, "Our little Andy doesn't know danger, yet, at all, hard as I'm trying to teach him. He's everywhere on this ranch that his little legs can carry him. I have to know every minute where he is and what he's doing until he's old enough to know what can hurt him, or not."

"I tell you, Jocey, we're all going to be fine. Now I really think it's time we all went to bed. Lot of hard work waiting for us tomorrow." He got to his feet, stretched and yawned. "Sure handy for me that Rom sees to the animals at night before turning in to his bed in the new bunkhouse."

She hesitated to agree. "My guess is that he's still up and teaching that mule another fool stunt down in the barn." She centered the salt and pepper shakers and sugar bowl on the table and brushed at a crumb she'd missed earlier. "Or plunking on that banjo he's trying to learn to play, with some help from Nila. I'm proud how hard he worked to buy it. Nearly wore out my Sears, Roebuck catalogue, though, before he had the two dollars and ninety-five cents the banjo cost." A fulfilling tiredness spread through her body. "It's a pretty thing, the nickel shell and calfskin head. I like the lively, happy sound that it makes. Does a lot to take away a body's cares, you know, if not the yen to dance up a storm." She laughed.

"He's with the banjo or the mule, either one or both, probably." Pete caught her shoulder and yawned. "Bedtime, honey." He gave her a pat as he headed for the other room to repeat his message there.

A few days later, Jocelyn folded the sun-dried towel she'd taken from the line and watched her neighbor, Mabel Goody, drive her horse and small buggy faster than normal up the lane, a dust trail billowing behind her. Placing the towel in her waiting basket and seeing that Andy was absorbed in racing his shadow back and forth in the yard, she walked to meet her company.

Mabel threw the lines aside and all but tumbled from the buggy. "You're going to be too late, Jocelyn, buyin' the Skiddy Livery. You'll hardly believe what I found out in town today, what all's going on behind your back." She removed a hanky from her reticule and mopped her sweating face.

"Come on back here and sit in the shade," Jocelyn pointed to a bench under the cottonwood tree a few feet away, "it's cooler in the backyard than in the house. I'll bring us some iced tea."

"Now then," she said a few minutes later, handing Mabel her tea and Andy a cup of cold milk. "What's going on? I sent a note right away for the mailman to deliver to Edna Ann, telling her that I'm buying the livery stable. That the decision is for sure."

"About everybody in town and roundabout for miles knows what you've decided, Jocelyn. But time is passing and you need to finish the deal with Edna Ann before this trouble explodes."

Jocelyn's jaw clenched in frustration. She took a deep breath. "Matters are moving as fast as can be, Mabel. I haven't been able to close the deal because Pete and I both want to pay cash as much as possible and it took a few days to sell a young bull and two older cows." She was silent a moment, gathering her thoughts. "The bank would probably give me the loan for the rest of what I need, without Pete's signing for it, too. In case not, I need him to be with me and I'm waiting for him to be ready to go."

"Elsa Noack and I were both sayin' in her store the other day that we knew if it was just you settlin' the deal it'd be fast as lightnin' follows thunder. I hate that us women are treated wrongly at times, like we don't have good sense and our man," she rolled her eyes. "the only one who can to take care of money matters. When many of us are a sight smarter than our husbands. Not that I'm saying that about my husband, Lyman. I'd say we're equal smart." She settled on the bench, her eyes on Andy playing duck and hide with his shadow. She gave Jocelyn's arm a sympathetic pat. "Sorry I interrupted, dear, go on with what you were sayin'."

"We plan to go to town day after tomorrow. Pete will be finished by then and we can leave things in Rom's hands here on the ranch for the short time we're gone. Now, tell me what's happened."

"It's them newcomers to Skiddy don't you know, the hat woman, Miss Rudd, and Jessop L. Cochran? They've become friends—well more than friends," she rolled her eyes, "if gossip is correct. Being of the same mind they intend to work together to halt your plans quick as scat. They've heard that you've decided to buy out Edna Ann and they're claimin' to everybody that not by a jugful will that happen."

"Why not? Edna Ann has my word, and we intend to finish the deal. They can't stop it."

"Well, they're blamed sure that they can. They've talked to other folks and some have overheard them at the café, all abuzz with their intentions. Maretta Rudd thinks it's fine for J.L. to buy poor Edna Ann out for a few dollars and use the land as he pleases." She leaned back in her chair, arms crossed on her ample bosom, eyes serious. "Another thing, he's trying to worm his way onto the town council and is sure he'll win the spot on the board Elsa Noack is vacating. Make a way for him to convince everybody to get rid of the livery business with little fuss."

"Honest?" For a moment she couldn't say more and the silence was heavy. Up by the barn a cowbell tinkled. Shay, the mule, brayed, "eeonk, eeonk, onk onk." Nearby, her chickens scratched for worms and clucked to announce their find to others.

"Yes, sorry to say. Maretta has pledged to aid him in gettin' picked, talks hard to womenfolk who visit her hat shop an' convinces them that when J.L. and his intentions come to a vote, they'd best make their husbands vote the right way, and the women vote for him, too."

"I hope the mayor and members of the council has better sense than to allow him to be a councilman," Jocelyn muttered under her breath. "Is anyone else running for Elsa's position, that you know of?"

"I heard that George Jacobsen is thinking on it, but also saying he's pretty busy at the feed store and might not have time for the council job."

"George would be a far better choice than this newcomer, J.L. Cochran. George is a good man, sociable, well-mannered, intelligent, and he cares about Skiddy."

"Other folks feel like that, too, thank heaven," Mabel said. "Blast Cochran's hide. He's the only person besides Maretta who owns a motorcar, his is a spidery-lookin' Oldsmobile he likes to brag on, putt-putt-puttin' up and down main street, hand on the horn to get more attention. He's sayin' that he'll immediately block your plans to buy and keep the livery operatin'. He intends to persuade the council to agree 'that the town must grow up to the times' turn to the motorcar and not be laggards. The spot where the livery is now, they're insistin' could become a 'fine establishment' selling Fords, and Oldsmobiles, and maybe them fancy new motorcars called 'Cadillacs'. They'll also have a business to service the machines, too, they claim."

"Edna Ann has told them that I intend to buy, hasn't she?" Jocelyn asked through a dry throat. She brushed a fly away from her face.

"More than once but they've been bullyin' her somethin' awful, anyways. Poor thing, she's prayin' to God that you'll come settle the matter right soon."

"We will, most certainly, and we'll put a fast stop to this troublemaking clatter."

FOUR

"Be careful," Mabel warned. She clutched her brown ruffled collar away from her throat and fanned herself with the other hand. "Maretta's been spreadin' around that she can easy talk you out of buyin' the livery stable."

Jocelyn laughed. "I doubt very much that she can do that. In a way, I admire Maretta Rudd, a woman alone operating a business. But I can't abide her intentions to destroy a perfectly good business that's needed by many more citizens than need her pretty hats. Nor can I appreciate her siding up with someone like Cockroach." She clapped her hand over her mouth, shocked that Prank's nickname for J.L. slipped out like butter on a hot potato. She clamped her lips to stop her giggles to no avail and eyed Mabel, hands clasped to her chest and laughing.

"Cockroach," Mabel choked out, "cockroach? If a name ever fit a person, that one sure fits Mr. Jessop Ludwig Cochran, fancy Dan that he is." She wiped her eyes, snickered. "How'd you ever come up with the bug nickname, Jocelyn?"

"Prank Morgan at the livery calls him that, says that is what J.L. was called where he came from." She sobered and scrubbed a hand over her face. "Using a mean nickname isn't something I'd usually do."

"Well, it is right enough for a nasty pest," Mabel defended, "that takes over and is blessed hard to get rid of, you know." She was silent a moment, crossing her arms over her chest. "I'm afraid folks've got a bigger problem with that man than they realize, sure enough. Polite and fine as he makes himself out to be, he's trouble." She turned a troubled stare in the direction of Skiddy.

"I'm afraid so, too, and it's no help that Miss Rudd is in cahoots with him. I'm going into town tomorrow and I'm going to pay Edna Ann in full for the livery stable business. I'm going to keep it running and," she smiled with calm confidence, "I grant you that nobody will do away with the livery, not now, not for a long, long time. On the side I'm going to buy and sell mules and pay back the bank loan. I'm going to take care of my family like I always have," her chin lifted, "and I expect they'll help me when I need it." She finished by echoing Pete, "And we're going to be fine."

Mabel, eyes bright and knowing, leaned toward Jocelyn and covered her hand with her own. "I expect you'll do all of that and teach them fool newcomers a thing or two. I don't have a doubt, from what I know of you." She stood up. "Now I need to head home and fix Lyman's supper. Good luck, tomorrow, and don't let them two beat you down a whit."

"I'll do my best to reason with them. That if they

want a motorcar business in Skiddy, they have to pick another piece of property." It was easy to say, how easy to make it happen remained to be seen. "Wait, Mabel, you said something about Edna Ann being bullied. She's handling it well enough, isn't she?" She took the empty cup Andy handed her and for a second or two watched him sneaking up on a Monarch butterfly landed in a patch of white poppy mallow. "Go ahead," she motioned to Mabel when the butterfly lifted into the air and Andy laid on his stomach in the grass.

"As much as possible. Maretta ordered poor Edna Ann to be patient, claiming that she and Mr. Cochran'll have the money she needs to start over. By the way, what they're offerin' is a small fraction of what Edna Ann is askin' and that you agreed to pay. If she wouldn't sell to them, they hinted that J.L. has a buyer with money to spare who is interested in the land and might pay her a little more."

A flush of anger climbed in Jocelyn's cheeks. "Not if I can help it. Do you know how Edna Ann took to their offer?" She scooted over on the bench and helped Andy climb up beside her. She hugged him close and motioned for Mabel to continue.

"Maretta's wrathiness left Edna Ann in tears. The woman called her a fool for not sellin' to J.L., claimed that the community's dawdlin' over the matter was bad enough, didn't need more from her. But Edna Ann cried mad tears. She was right proud that she stood up for herself and she'll do as she pleases with property that belongs to her. A business that had meant every-thing to her poor dead husband."

"Good." Jocelyn felt better. She rose from the bench, holding Andy's hand as he jumped down.

Mabel leaned to take his face in her hands and kiss his cheek. "My special boy. Mind your mama, now. I know you will." She said to Jocelyn, "If there's anything I can do to help, let me know. The little one here, can stay with me if there's a time you need someone to look after him."

"Thank you, Mabel, I'll keep that in mind. Mmm... would tomorrow be all right?" Midwife to the community's women, and Jocelyn's neighbor, Mabel had helped bring Andy into the world. She loved her many 'special children' and they loved her.

"Sure thing, I'd love to have him stay with me. Bring him over, or I can take Andy with me now."

Jocelyn leaned down and pulled him back against her knees. "Pete and I will drop him off in the morning before we drive to Skiddy, but thank you."

"Bye, Mrs. Mabel," Andy called, running after the buggy as Mabel turned it in the lane to leave. He stopped and waved, then looked back at Jocelyn. "I can go to Mrs. Mabel's house tomorrow, right?"

"You can, but now Mama needs your help fixing supper for Daddy, Nila, and Rommy."

"Let's fix radishes and salt." He looked up, confident in his suggestion.

"Fine. Radishes and salt." She poised to run. "Race me to the garden."

～

Leaving their mule team, Alice and Zenith, with feed and water in the livery's wagon yard, Jocelyn and Pete strolled arm in arm toward the Skiddy bank. They were almost to the bank's entrance when a loud, unimaginable noise, 'oo-gah, oogah' blasted behind them, ambushing the morning quiet. "What in the name of Hannah...?" Jocelyn jerked to look. Maretta Rudd's brilliant red Model A Ford chugged and coughed along the dusty street, setting dogs barking and horses tied to railings pulling to be free. Maretta, her nose in the air, a blue platter-of-a-hat cleverly piled thick with purple ribbon roses, and her hand on the horn, made another ear-splitting 'oo-gah, oo-gah, oo-gah'. Along the street people stopped to stare. Not a few planted hands to their ears and glared.

"What...!" Jocelyn exclaimed when she caught Pete's wide grin in that direction and a tip of his hat to Maretta.

"Just puttin' a little of the fire out."

"We can hope so." Jocelyn smothered a laugh as they entered the bank moments later. "But never mind about Miss Rudd at the moment. I'm excited, Pete, and so glad we're doing this."

"Now if the banker will see things our way," Pete muttered back at her. Eyebrow quirked and a hand on her elbow, they moved past the teller's cage toward the bank manager's cubbyhole office.

"I don't know why he wouldn't."

"Hope you folks are having a fine day?" The bank manager, a large, well-built man with a neat brown beard and moustache, shook their hands and motioned them toward two oak chairs facing his somewhat battered but tidy desk, while he took his chair behind it. It seemed like forever to Jocelyn, though it was more likely thirty or forty minutes, that the three of them went detail by detail over the ranch's value at present and considerations of the future. She sat forward with pounding heart and her mouth dry as further attention was given to the value and importance of the Skiddy Livery Stable business. When finished, she looked expectantly at the bank manager.

"I don't see nary a problem here, folks." Stroking his beard, the good-natured banker smiled wide at them. "The livery is a busy, thriving business, and with the mule sales you're planning that should take care of the payments in good time. Congratulations." Again he shook their hands. "Glad to see the business is going to you, and not another fella that's been looking at it."

"Would that be Mr. J.L. Cochran?" Jocelyn asked quietly.

"Oh, you know about that? Yessir," he leaned back in his chair. "J.L. Cochran intended to have it. He looked at other spots in town for this motorcar business he's planning. He was laughed at for the price he wanted to pay—and the bank is not about to make him another loan 'til he pays on loans he has already on other businesses." He stood. "Wait here and I'll have a clerk draw up the papers for you to sign." He nodded toward the ornate, cast iron double glass inkwell with pen rests, that centered his desk and Jocelyn had been admiring.

"I hadn't heard that J.L. tried for other properties to build his motorcar business." Jocelyn stated later, watching Pete sign the loan papers, having had her turn. "But I'm not surprised he wasn't taken seriously. He badgered Edna Ann—Mrs. Lockhart, something awful trying to make her accept his puny offer to buy the livery."

"Yep." The bank manager replaced the ink pen in its holder and folded his arms across his chest. "The cheapskate thought it'd be easy to talk a poor lonely widow into selling out to him for pennies. Lucky for the dear woman that you folks came into the picture."

Pete chuckled. "You don't fool these ladies." He took Jocelyn's elbow, smiling proudly down at her as they headed for the door.

An hour later they sat in Edna Ann's small parlor, drinking coffee and celebrating the signing of their loan, the livery now the same as theirs. "Maretta Rudd," Edna Ann hesitated to take a sip of coffee, "scorched my ears plenty trying to stop me from selling to you folks. Mr. Cochran did the same, talked smooth as cream gravy. Claiming he'd be doing me a huge favor, taking the livery off my hands. I know a sharpy and a liar when I hear one—besides offering me a fraction of what the business is worth. Turned them both down and they sure didn't like it. It's a relief to leave town, the way they feel toward me and my plans for Carl's livery." She frowned. "They said they weren't finished. That worries me some. You know, about what they might try when it's turned over to you, Jocelyn."

Jocelyn gave a slight nod. "We'll face that when it comes. I don't doubt that there'll be trouble from them up to the moment it's made clear they've truly lost. I'm sorry we weren't able to complete the sale sooner, save you from their badgering." After a moment Jocelyn continued with a smile, lifting her cup, "But it's done now, and I couldn't be happier to be the new owner, and help you out at the same time."

Pete spoke, "Those two hifalutin' city folk just don't understand that it'll be a hell—pardon my English—of a long time before expensive motorcars replace mules and horses altogether, if ever. In the meantime, Jocey'll be showing these folks a thing or two, she'll boss this livery business just fine."

Edna Ann's eyes sparkled with excitement. "I'd wanted so much for things to turn out this way, Jocelyn, and I started packing as soon as I got your note that you were buying the livery." Looking thoughtful, she replaced her cup in its saucer and nodded. "I know in my heart that, Carl, too, would've favored you to be the one to own his livery. And heaven knows, if he were alive, he wouldn't for a minute stand for the livery to be done away with, when so many people are dependent on it."

"I'm guessing he'd be proud that his old friend from the war, Prank Morgan, is running it now," Pete added.

"Oh, he would, he would." Edna Ann wiped her eyes, smiling through tears.

~

Two days later, Jocelyn was back at the livery with little Andy and Rom, the latter there to help Prank rebuild a stall that a visiting stallion had kicked to pieces, and to do other chores. She put Andy at play in the livery office, building his own livery from small pieces of wood, while she went over the business ledger, at times needing to squint to make out Prank's penciled facts and figures and smiling at the comments he occasionally scribbled in. Short details about the "fool dude" who wanted to rent a mount to carry him all the way from Skiddy to Wichita. One-way rentals were simply not done by any livery, there being no way to retrieve the horse. If the customer wanted to buy the horse and saddle, they might discuss that. In this case, the dude wasn't interested beyond a one-way ride. Prank probably convinced him to beg a ride on a freight wagon or some such if he could get one.

When satisfied with her readings in the ledger, clarifying some with her own figures, Jocelyn, with Andy in hand, watched work on the new stall, then strolled the pastures out back. She found a few yards of fencing starting to sag, no doubt from a horse leaning into it. She pulled it back but it didn't stay. She peeked into the hay barn, thinking not for the first time, that rearranging it would make a fine place to hold mule sales.

"You're doing a good job, fellas," she told Prank and Rom when she was back inside the livery. "There's some saggy fence outside, south pasture, that needs tightening up again, if not replaced with something stronger. Not sagging badly, but you never know when another critter will take advantage of what's started. I'll likely be pasturing a few mules briefly, between sale times, and we don't want them pushing over fence to wander loose around town. Some folks," in her mind she pictured Maretta and J.L. Cochran, "will likely as not fuss that they are a nuisance as it is. Blame their souls."

"We'll be fixin' the fence, won't we, boy?" Prank addressed Rom. "You can bet your bottom dollar on that, Missus Pladson. Dontcha worry." He gave the rising board wall of the new stall a pat, and went to wait on customers, a pretty young girl and a handsome fellow carrying a picnic basket, who'd just come into the livery barn.

Jocelyn smiled, watching Prank fit them out with a prancy horse and a wagon—Rom had recently given the wagon wheels a fresh coat of yellow paint—teasing and telling them to have a good time, and accepting their three-dollar payment.

It's just natural there will be ups and down in my new business, and I'm ready for that. For now, Jocelyn took deep, satisfied breaths, feeling like she owned the world. Prank returned to the stall project and she told him, and Rom, "I'm going to Noack's General Store now, and order a block of salt to be delivered for our back pasture here. I'll stop, too, to tell Edna Ann good-bye. She leaves early tomorrow on the morning train, the first leg of her trip to Louisiana."

"You wanta' leave the little button here with me while you're a'doin' that?" Rom asked.

"No, Son, he's going with me. He'll like the walk and visiting folks at the store. I expect I'll buy him an ice cream which, hot as it is, he'll have to finish on the spot."

Andy began to bounce in place hearing of ice cream. Smiling wide, he caught his mother's hand and pulled.

"All right, all right," she said, "I'm coming, Andy

❧

Jocelyn stepped a little faster passing MISS MARETTA'S MILLINERY and its window displaying large feathered and flowered hats. A quick peek and she was relieved to see Maretta busy with two lady customers that Jocelyn didn't recognize. At a table and mirror, the women were swapping hats back and forth, trying on the enormous, platter-sized confections. Elise Botts, a freckle-faced, strawberry blonde friend of Nila's, who worked part time at the hat shop, was dusting inside the window. She smiled and lifted a hand to Jocelyn and Andy. Jocelyn waved back. She was pleased Nila had become friends with such a nice young woman. The two had become as close as sisters in the past few years.

"I'm so glad to hear that you've bought the livery from Edna Ann," Mrs. Noack said as she waited on Jocelyn, adding the salt block to her tab. "Many of us town-folk were worried sick the blessed matter might go the other way, the livery an' the big old hay barn torn down with nowhere for out-of-towners to stable their horses, or towners to rent a team and wagon. Such foolery," she shook her head, "talk about everybody owning an expensive motorcar of a sudden."

"I agree, pretty crazy talk it was and is," Jocelyn replied. "But I'm the owner now, and the livery is here to stay as long as it is needed." She looked down at Andy, furiously licking his ice cream to keep it from dripping still more on his hand.

"Here's a cloth to wipe the boy's hands and face." Mrs. Noack smiled and handed her a scrap of calico, adding, "You are a godsend, Jocelyn, helping make possible Edna Ann's move to be with her family."

"It was my pleasure, and owning a mule trading business has been in the back of my mind, anyway, for a long time. Before we leave for home, the boy and I are going to drop by her house to tell Edna Ann goodbye and to wish her a safe trip."

Walking back from the store toward the livery and Edna Ann's house and coming even with MISS MARETTA'S MILLINER, Jocelyn heard, through an open window to the left of the door, a woman's shrill voice and a deeper male voice entangled in an undeci-

pherable argument inside the hat shop. At mention of
her name "that Pladson woman" she halted, lips
clamped, and backed a few steps to listen, pulling Andy
with her.

"You didn't do enough to stop her," Maretta was
screeching, loud enough, Jocelyn thought, to be heard
plumb in Geary County. "Not enough, soon enough,
and now see what that Pladson woman has done! She's
bought the livery outright, the whole smelly business,
and means to keep it running. Dear God, how could
you, J.L.? We would've won, we could've done away
with that smelly place like it'd never been. Had a business that could make us both barrels of money, selling
motorcars—being the first such business to set up in this
part of Kansas."

"Dear woman, calm down," J.L. barked, gentleman
politeness momentarily abandoned. "I did what I could.
We aren't going to sit back like sleeping frogs on a rock.
We won't settle for what's happened." His voice lifted.
"It's a grand new day for transportation. We can put
that country bumpkin out of business before she knows
what's happened to her. It's going to take time, anyway,
to put together the money, find the right investors, to
stake the motorcar business. Be patient, dear lady," he
rasped, "patient."

From inside there was a sudden loud *thwack*
followed by J.L.'s loud throaty yelp. *In the name of
Hannah, had Maretta struck him with something?*

Jocelyn hesitated, held her breath, pulled little
Andy closer to her, holding her hands over his ears,
knowing she should move on for her son's benefit, but
also wanting to hear more of this argument that had so
very much to do with her personally.

"Don't tell me what to do!" Maretta screeched. "I've been patient, taking your word that you could prevent this calamity. I told you that I had valuable jewelry to sell, as my portion in starting the business. I never should have listened to you, you fool."

Peeking through the window, Jocelyn noted that Maretta's face was a mottled, vibrant pink, swollen all out of proportion. Jocelyn's hand went to her own face. Had J.L. done this to her, struck her? *Sweet Hannah, if so, he was an even more terrible person than she'd thought.* No matter, whatever happened in that situation it wasn't exactly her business, but she had to stop them from thinking they could destroy her plans. They would not put her out of business. Never. She stepped toward the door to the store, heart pounding as she reached for the knob.

FIVE

The door to the hat shop ripped from Jocelyn's fingers. J.L., stooped, both hands to his head, lunged through the open door. Maretta followed, furiously swinging a ladies' hat mannequin by the neck, the head part broken off. White plaster chips of the missing head flew from J.L.'s hair and speckled his shoulders and front of his shirt. A fine grey fedora whizzed by Jocelyn's face.

J.L.'s large body hit Jocelyn hard getting by her. She stumbled backward on the boardwalk and almost went down, losing Andy's hand. He hit the plank walk on his face, hard. She leaped to pick him up, hugged him tight. With her hand she wiped at his tears, the dirt and scratches on his face. "That man shouldn't have bumped into us like that, Andy, but you'll be fine. Momma is so sorry." She kissed him and fought her own tears.

She glared after J.L. who'd fetched his fedora, clamped it on and hustled down the street away from Maretta. Possibly in the heat of the moment unaware that he'd nearly knocked her down, and caused hurt to her boy. She started to leave, then noticed Maretta in the doorway glaring at her. A tremor of shock raced over Jocelyn, at sight of Maretta's face close up. Hitting a woman was dead wrong, if J.L. was the culprit guilty of whatever took place. Jocelyn clutched at her own face and motioned toward Maretta's. "Did Mr. Cochran do that to you—he hits you?"

Maretta scowled, her face resembling an angered, swollen-faced cat. She hissed, "Shut up! It's none of your business." The door banged in Jocelyn's face.

Gritting her teeth, Jocelyn wished she'd kept going rather than expose Andy to the explosion between Maretta and J.L. She picked up her son and hurried along the street toward Edna's Ann's house.

"That lady isn't nice, is she?" Andy twisted in her arms to look at her, his squinty-eyed little face too serious.

Jocelyn hesitated, sighing. "I think she was feeling peaky and couldn't help herself." She kissed his poor little scratched face. "But we won't let that bother us." She forced gaiety into her voice. "We're going to see Edna Ann, and the kittens. You'll like that, won't you?" She turned the corner off Main Street toward Edna Ann's house, feeling regretful that this would be the last time she'd see her friend. Glad, though, to be shed of Cochran's and Maretta's efforts to halt her buying the livery. That, thank Hannah, was done.

~

"I thought I was just going to have to walk away from this little house, abandon it," Edna Ann was saying as she led Jocelyn and Andy inside. She nodded and looked around, motioning at the small, apple blossom-wallpapered room, the simple walnut furniture. "It isn't much but I loved it, life here with Carl. Thankfully," she briefly pressed two fingers to her smiling lips, "at the last minute, friends of the Noacks over to the store, made an offer to buy my house. Not a lot of money but more than nothing."

"I'm glad for you." Jocelyn gave her a hug.

While Andy played with the growing kittens—which Jocelyn had promised earlier to take out to the ranch—she quietly described to Edna Ann what had happened at the hat shop. "You should have seen Maretta's face," she finished, experiencing a slight chill, "swollen, lumpy and red. I wondered if J.L. has been hitting her? As much as I don't care for him, he doesn't seem the kind and Maretta wasn't about to say, though I tried to ask."

Edna Ann wiped at her mouth and looked down at her feet for a minute. Recovered, she clutched Jocelyn's arm. "No, that's not what happened to Maretta at all." Her eyes twinkled with good humor and she struggled not to laugh.

"What then? Do you know?"

She nodded, laughing softly. "Oh, yes, I know. It's terrible of me to laugh about it, but it strikes me funny an' I can't help it. Mites, fleas, or some other kind of bugs, came in an order of ostrich feathers for Maretta's hat making."

"Sweet Hannah, no." Jocelyn clapped a hand over her mouth.

"Yes. And the second large box that had other bird's wings, plumes, and feathered breasts wasn't infested, so I heard. Those are bug bites on Maretta Rudd's face, Jocelyn, and from what I've heard she was bitten practically all over."

Jocelyn chewed her lip to stifle a giggle and sat back in her chair, experiencing a moment's gratification, but sympathy, too. The poor woman. Bug bites. She'd been right, then, telling Andy that the 'lady not being nice' was due to her being 'peaky'. Not that Maretta wasn't furious about failing to have her way about the livery, too, but no need to go into that. She decided to change the subject. "You must be so excited, moving to be near your sister and in a whole different place from Kansas."

"Oh, my, yes." She leaned to clasp Jocelyn's arm. "My sister has written to tell me the treats she has in store. So many firsts for me: dishes with names like 'gumbo, crawfish, and jambalaya'. She says I'll like them but I don't know about that, I'll find out when I get there. In the bayou country she says folks like frog legs and turtle soup—don't think I'll like either one of those but you never know. Can hardly wait to try the desserts she wrote me about: beignets which are really doughnuts but square, and delicious. Sweet potato pie, pecan pie, and bread pudding with rum sauce." She sat back, clapping her hands together.

"You're making me hungry, Edna Ann."

She chuckled and continued. "I look forward to seeing the beautiful plantations—" she hesitated, "but I don't abide slavery—I'm glad that's over. So much to see —Louisiana has those beautiful magnolia flowers, like

Kansas has the sunflower. Parades and festivals like the Mardi Gras." She gave a happy sigh. "My life is going to be different, but I have a feeling that I'll love it all, especially being with my younger sister, her family."

"I know that you will, Edna Ann, and I couldn't be happier for you." In another few minutes, Jocelyn stood, calling to Andy still playing with the kittens in the kitchen, "Time for us to head on home, Son."

"I have a basket to put the kittens in," Edna Ann said, jumping up. She brought the basket and handed the mother cat to Jocelyn.

That done, the women hugged goodbye. "I know I've said it already a dozen times, but I'm so happy for you, Edna Ann, I know you're going to have a wonderful new start in Louisiana with your sister and her family, the new baby. But I'm going to miss you something fierce. Please write to me, and I'll write to you."

"I will." Edna Ann gave Andy a hug and handed him the basket of squirming kittens. She was beginning to tear up. "I'm going to miss you, too, Jocelyn Pladson. You've been so good to me, taking the livery off my hands so I could do this. Problem is, I think I've handed you a passel of trouble at the same time." Her voice was strained and her brow wrinkled as she continued, "I don't think J.L. Cochran and Maretta Rudd are going to give up their intentions to replace the livery with a motorcar business. Heaven knows what they might do, to get their way. I don't think I could stand it if they did you serious wrong, hurt you. We don't know either one of them well enough."

Jocelyn's stomach flip flopped. "I know you're right, but I can handle them. I can."

~

It's silly, Jocelyn told herself, *to be so proud of words on a thin board*, 'WE NOW BUY AND SELL MULES—SKIDDY LIVERY STABLE AND MULE BARN—Jocelyn Royal Pladson, Proprietor'. She was fiercely proud of them as she placed them in the wagon, and that was that. With Nila and Rom's help, the three of them had finished a dozen board signs to distribute around town and nail to fence posts. The paper signs they'd made from paper scraps, given them free by the newspaper office, had nearly all been ripped down by some sneak or other. The same message had been painted in white, four-foot-high letters over the wide red doors of the livery barn. *Nothing anybody could do to change a blame thing about that sign.* She was finally, almost able, to drive to the livery without looking up giddy with excitement.

Driving to Skiddy with the new signs, Rom holding the reins, Jocelyn noted that he was deep in thought about something making him grin. "What's on your mind, Son? That's making you look happy?"

"Ol' Prank. That fella tells the best stories," Rom mused in his crackling teenage voice.

She motioned for him to continue.

"I dunno for sure why," he looked at her, "but when Prank spins a yarn, I feel like I was there. In the Union's war with the South, I mean. I swear I can hear the cannon, feel the burn of Minnie balls just missin' me. The smoke." He was silent a moment, thinking. "My stomach rumbles with hunger for them tomatoey pork and beans in a can that a man named Van Camp come up with, to feed soldiers easy. Like they don't have to cook 'em, just eat 'em from the can."

"Really? I don't think I've heard about that. Pork and beans in a can, ready to eat as they are. That's a good thing, for those soldiers."

"Durn right." He continued, "I swear I can feel the ache in my legs I'm so tired from marching, when the old man tells it. The scrapes and tears to my skin from dartin' in deep woods hidin' and comin' up on the enemy." His voice choked with emotion, "I wouldn't miss that old man's war stories for nothin'. Even if the south lost that battle at Wilson Creek to the Union."

"I'm sure he appreciates your listening to them." Jocelyn chuckled and patted his knee. "I think it is wonderful, for the two of you, but I wouldn't want the storytelling to interfere with your work, Son, or Prank's."

"It don't. I'll show you today that we've finished a lotta chores that you had on your list an' right along with runnin' the livery business. Now and then a fella or two will drop in for a visit an' maybe hear Prank's stories. But they don't stop our work, sometimes they pitch in and help, even. Curryin', feedin', and waterin' the horses, scoopin' the floors."

"You like working with Prank at the livery, then?"

"Best job I'll probably ever have, Ma, until I get my own ranch someday. Can't say as I like the ribbin' I get for havin' a lady boss, though," he grinned, teasing her, "but I accuse them jokers of bein' jealous and tryin' to get my job. Everybody laughs about that."

Her heart warmed when he called her 'Ma'. Over time, Rom and Nila had become more than somebody's else's children that they'd taken in. They were family, and much loved.

Following a brief chat with Prank at the livery about preparing for hay to be delivered from the ranch, soon, and a few minutes with the ledger going over business since the last time she was in town, Jocelyn headed to the post office to put up one of her last paper signs on the notice board there, with the postmaster's approval. She was tacking it up when she heard footsteps behind her, felt someone standing close, breathing on the back of her neck and smelling of cigar smoke, an odor similar to burning straw.

Frowning, a quiver in her stomach, she stepped to the side and turned to look. "Hello, Mr. Cochran," she moved further from his bulk and said as civilly as she could manage, "I trust you're having a good day?"

"It's improved, seeing you today, Mrs. Pladson." He lipped the cigar around in his mouth and touched his hat in a grand gesture. "I've been looking for a chance to congratulate you." He removed the cigar and pointed it toward the flyer she'd tacked up. "I wish you success— but I'm concerned that that won't happen. Sorry. Truly, I am sorry." His wide, apologetic smile, showing his yellow tobacco-stained teeth, was as fake as a day-old flapjack pretending to be a three-layer Kentucky jam cake.

Sorry my foot.

"I don't need your concern, Mr. Cochran, or anybody else's for that matter." His fancy suit reeked so badly of cigar smoke that it was all she could to not cover her nose.

"Really? Let's hope," he winked at her, "that you

haven't put your husband's money into a big mistake. That wouldn't do now, would it?"

Our money. No mistake. She remained calm and smiled at him. Silent, waiting for him to read her mind and move his despicable self from her presence. Softly, the clock on the wall behind her ticked the minutes away.

Waiting for her answer and getting none, he breathed hard and veins stood out on his reddened neck. His lips flattened and she was sure he'd like to strangle her—if there'd been no witnesses around. "You'll see, Mrs. Pladson, that you have a lot to learn. Before you fail." There was an edge to his soft chuckle. He jabbed the well-chewed cigar back in his mouth, tipped his hat in tight fingers, and strode from the post office.

"Was Cochran bothering you, Mrs. Pladson?" the postmaster, Mr. Belshaw, one of her favorite Skiddy businessmen, came over to ask.

She took a deep breath. "It's a little thing, maybe, but I'm sure he'd have torn down my flyer, the sign," she nodded toward it, "as soon as I left here. He hates the fact that I will keep the livery and spoil his plans for a motorcar business in the livery's place. The truth is," she rubbed her brow and crossed her arms tightly, "many of the paper flyers have been ripped down as fast as my family can put them up. We're using wood signs and strong nails, now." She bit her lip. "Though that may not work much better. J.L. Cochran is a man of mean intent."

He frowned and stroked his beard. "I'll try to keep watch and see that nothing like that happens here. I know for a fact that other merchants in town are wanting the livery stable. Wanting it to be in force as many years yet as possible. And they appreciate you being the one in charge." He held out his hand, "Congratulations, by the way, Mrs. Pladson."

The tension she'd felt facing up to J.L. Cochran was fading and she shook the postmaster's hand. "Thank you so much, Mr. Belshaw." She took a deep breath. "I'd better be off, I'm taking one of our signs to Jacobsen's Feed and Seed Store next."

The postmaster smiled. "He'll display your sign, no trouble."

"I think so, too. George Jacobsen has always been fair with us. We intend to provide the livery as much oats and hay as we can spare from what we grow to feed home stock, but we buy seed, farm tools, and whatnot from Jacobsen's, doing our part keeping him in business. I'm sure that he'll do right by the sign." She wiggled her eyebrows and quipped, "Motorcars don't run on oats and hay. George's business is needed, too."

"I know what you mean and no, ma'am, they don't." He smiled and waved as she headed for the door.

After leaving a sign at the feed store, and then a stop at the *Skiddy Review* to place an ad seeking mule business, trade-sale-or boarding, Jocelyn headed back toward the livery for her team and wagon and the trip home. Having decided for Rom to stay in town for a few days and help Prank, she'd leave him a blanket from the wagon for sleeping in the livery's hayloft. Not for the first time, and not the last.

Moments later, feeling satisfied and her mind busy, she wasn't aware that she was passing the hat shop until Maretta suddenly stepped out and blocked her way. A slight shiver raced along Jocelyn's spine at the cold expression in Maretta's eyes. Had J.L. let her know that Jocelyn was in town, with a suggestion to ambush her?

"How's business?" Maretta's smile was more a grimace.

Jocelyn's shoulders pushed back and she looked Maretta in the eye. "Well enough, and about to get better with my mule sales added to livery services. Why do you ask?" Her heart seemed to thump loud in her ears, waiting.

"To warn you. If you think what you're doing will hold good you're badly mistaken. The old ways of transportation are the same as ended, doomed. The sooner you realize that, the better off you'll be, Mrs. Pladson. I hate to see you putting money and effort in a smelly, useless, cause. I intend, with every fiber of my body, to see your livery business torn down, over with, gone—to make way for progress, a new beginning."

"I intend for it to be operating here in Skiddy for the next twenty to forty years."

Maretta's brow wrinkled in distaste, color climbed in her face and her hands gripped her waist. "I don't understand—livery, mules? You, a woman. It's idiocy. Where is your shame, neglecting your family to tend this ridiculous, old-timey business?"

"It's not necessary for you to understand, Miss Rudd." Her voice was tight, but she still managed the dregs of a smile. "You only need to keep your nose out of my doings and let this matter be. I have other tasks to tend to now, I have to go." She took two steps, Maretta grabbed her arm, squeezing it painfully. Jocelyn looked at her, surprised, and twisted free. "In the name of Hannah, stop it. What're you thinking?" Across Maretta's shoulder she caught Elise staring at them from inside the shop.

Maretta grabbed her again. "I'm thinking to see you ruined, and back home where you belong. When that happens, you can thank me!"

"I'm sorry, Miss Rudd." Jocelyn jerked away. "You couldn't be more wrong."

Behind Maretta, Elise was vigorously nodding yes, with an encouraging smile in Jocelyn's direction.

With a deep satisfied breath, Jocelyn gave a discrete nod to Elise, gave Maretta her back, and continued down the street. Ignoring as best she could her wobbly knees and the scorching glare that followed her.

Six

Jocelyn was approaching the livery stable when she whirled and headed back to the hat shop. Maretta was startled to see her come through the door, and her frown deepened. She held the largest hat, of yellow straw, that Jocelyn had ever seen. With a threaded needle, she looked to be attaching an enormous clutch of artificial red roses, greenery, and silver ribbons to what Jocelyn supposed was called a *chateau*. Maretta set her work aside. She wore a dark look, her mouth curled with dislike. "What do you want, Jocelyn Pladson, why are you here?"

She took a deep breath. *Thank Hannah she didn't pick up those scissors and come at me with them.* "Miss Rudd, I want to apologize for my part in our fuss a few minutes ago. I'm sorry that we don't agree about my livery business—sorry that it's such a bother to your business here. May I ask why, in the first place, did you start up a new business in this spot, in this town, if you're not happy with the way things are?" She had surprised Maretta with her question, which pleased Jocelyn not a trifle.

For a second it appeared Maretta wasn't about to answer. Then, tightlipped, belligerent, she said, "This building was the only one the right size for my business that was available. And," she flipped a hand, "I was told through an acquaintance of the railroad magnate, Francis Skiddy, that this was an 'up and coming town, ripe for new business'. That is far from the truth, but even so, Mr. Cochran and I believe there is a chance to make it fact. A blind man could see that there's no end to improvements this town could use. That's why your livery stable has to go."

Jocelyn looked at her for a long moment, her shoulders dropped. At the door she hesitated, and turned. "I'm still sorry we can't agree." *And not for another blessed thing.*

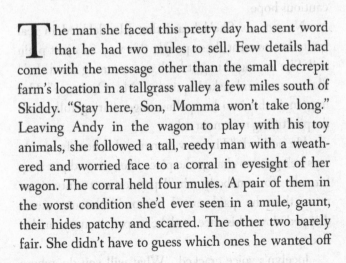

The man she faced this pretty day had sent word that he had two mules to sell. Few details had come with the message other than the small decrepit farm's location in a tallgrass valley a few miles south of Skiddy. "Stay here, Son, Momma won't take long." Leaving Andy in the wagon to play with his toy animals, she followed a tall, reedy man with a weathered and worried face to a corral in eyesight of her wagon. The corral held four mules. A pair of them in the worst condition she'd ever seen in a mule, gaunt, their hides patchy and scarred. The other two barely fair. She didn't have to guess which ones he wanted off his hands. She asked, anyway, "Which ones do you want to sell, Mr. ...?"

"Ivers, name's Ivers. Them two," he pointed at the scraggly animals, "the brown molly mule and that there grey draft mule. Good mules," he said, trying to sound convincing while he looked away. "Had a little trouble with blowflies eatin' at 'em, but they'll get over that."

He looked back at her and she shook her head, made her doubt clear with a frown. If Mr. Ivers thought he could fool her because she was a woman, he was dead wrong. He continued. "It's gotta be them two, Missus. I need them other two for travel. Me, my wife and childurn," his gaze darted toward a gaunt-faced woman and five ragged, barefoot youngsters watching hopefully from a short distance, "been evicted from this here farm. Was supposed to be off this place ten days ago, have to be gone by sundown tomorrow. Mr. Cochran said he'd get the law to run us off if we ain't." He scratched his head and waited. Licked his lip with cautious hope.

No, no, no. She'd heard that J.L. dabbled in real estate but to treat these people this way was just plain evil. She managed to grit back a very strong word she'd like to use and asked quietly, "Mr. Cochran?" Her fingernails bit into her palms, anger flaring full steam despite trying to remain calm.

He nodded. "The new owner a' this here farm. He says he's goin' to change the place like new and put it up for sale. To somebody who'll pay ten or twenty times more than he paid me, I reckon." Nervous sweat dripped down his face and he wiped it away on his sleeve.

Jocelyn's voice cracked, "What will you do, where

will you go?" Her glance dragged again to his family. Then to Andy who still played busily in the wagon.

"Me and the wife decided to try our luck further west." He shrugged and spit. "We'll work our way 'til we find somethin' we can stay at for good, somethin' of our own."

"Those mules are in terrible shape and you know it, Mr.—Ivers. Nobody but a fool or a blind man would buy them. Even so—" She began to feel drained. *Maybe a well-trained vet could turn them around, but probably not. Blow-fly infection was near impossible to cure and it wouldn't be surprising if the mules died. They looked close to doing so already.*

After another fifteen minutes of back and forth discussion, moments of silence, plagued with sympathy for the man and his family waiting stone still, not to mention the infested mules, dealing with Andy's restlessness at her side and wanting to leave, she surrendered and asked him his price. "Mr. Ivers, the mules are nowhere near that valuable. Especially the state they're in." She started toward her wagon, Andy in hand.

"Fifteen dollars apiece?" he said gruffly to her back.

She sighed and turned. "That'll do." She handed him forty dollars, then added ten more and smiled, "Keep it, and good luck Mr. Ivers." With a lump in her throat, she waved to his wife and children.

~

Feeling sick with misgivings, Jocelyn tied the mules to the back of her wagon. *Her first buy and she'd dealt with her heart, not her head. She felt like a fool.* Still, she reasoned as she drove back toward Skiddy, she'd done the poor man and his family a good deed where no one else was doing so—especially not that scoundrel, J.L. Cochran. As they rolled along, she gave Andy a biscuit and a piece of bacon she'd brought along for when he got hungry and he was happy as a bear cub with a honeycomb, licking his lips, bouncing up and down on the wagon seat. Life could be worse.

Back in Skiddy at the livery, the pathetic mules were turned into the pen of lush, waiting pasture. "What do you think?" Jocelyn asked Prank. He was holding Andy, clamping his lips as he tried not to laugh, eyes wide.

She stood her ground. "Don't laugh. If there is a way to make them healthy, I want to know what it is."

Prank sobered, put Andy down to play in the grass. He walked over to the closest mule, checked inside its mouth, rubbed at its hide, ran his hand down its legs. "The worst," he said, "is that they're sufferin' blow-fly larvae buried in their hide. We can treat that with coal oil and see what it'll do. A good vet might have some idees that'll help. Lord knows they got some good grass here to graze, and fatten up on. They ain't dead yet, Missus, so we got us something to work on, leastwise." His words were encouraging, the expression on his face less so. "It'll take time, but I think we gotta chance of turnin' them into good, saleable mules."

Jocelyn was enough relieved she didn't know whether to whoop or cry. Instead, she hugged Prank. "I'm so glad I have you to help me, Prank, I can't thank you enough."

He "harrumphed" and gave her back a pat, his face burning.

Finishing up a few small further chores at the

livery, almost ready to leave for home, she was taking a last look at the pathetic mules—happy to see one ambling slowly toward the trough, another beginning to graze—when J.L. Cochran swaggered up. From the gleeful look pasted on his face, she surmised that he'd seen her arrival back in Skiddy from his hardware store's window. "Are you in the business of mule sales or mule burials?" he taunted, "they look too sick to even graze." He shook his head in pity. "What did you pay for them? If it was more than a penny a piece you got robbed." He chuckled. "My yes, how about a wager whether they survive or not?" He reached for his vest pocket. "My bet is they won't last more than another week, at most." He pointed at a mule that stood with its head almost to the ground, and he pulled out a sheaf of bills. "How about it, Mrs. Pladson? Want to bet?"

Word of his gambling on just about anything had spread aplenty. She gave him a scathing look. "You'd lose, Mr. Cochran. Put your money away." She wanted away from here, hated his presence, looked around for Andy and spotted him just inside the livery door, playing on a stack of hay bundles.

"Ah, well, maybe not today," Cochran mumbled with a shake of his head. Seeing that his offer was going nowhere, he moved up close and with fake apology in his eyes added, "Just joking, anyhow, Mrs. Pladson, just joking." He put the money away, chomped down on his cigar and blew the smoke through his nose.

The foul smell of it flooded her face. Jaw clenched, she jerked back, swatting the air in front of her.

"No need to get so serious, Mrs. Pladson." He held his cigar away. "It just appears to me that you made a sorry buy is all."

Damn him! "You know perfectly well where these mules came from J.L." *Cockroach.* "And you know what a cruel thing you did to that poor family, putting them out of house and home. Yes, I helped them. I gave them money they needed badly and I don't care a whit that I bought mules in poor shape. I'm glad that I did what I did, and Prank and I can worry about the mules and what we'll do to heal them, make them fat and healthy. Wait and see!" *Cockroach.*

"Please, don't get upset. I felt sorry for the Ivers family, that's why I helped them by buying that rundown property." His chest puffed out and wearing a cocky, satisfied smile he flicked the ashes from his cigar.

Bald-faced lie. You practically stole that farm is what. And if I had something at hand to hit you with, I'd knock that toothy smile to the back of your worthless head.

"I feel intense sympathy for you, honestly, Mrs. Pladson," he was saying, his expression radiating superiority. "I'd sympathize with any woman trying to run a livery business, along with mule trading and selling. What's happened here," he looked pointedly at the gaunt mules beginning to graze, "is proof that it's simply not proper for a woman to run a business—or attempt to."

He actually had the gall to look proud of his wise and noble conclusions, raising her ire practically to the boiling point.

She bit the words off, "Maretta Rudd is a business woman, isn't she? Elsa Noack operates their mercantile, along with her husband, besides being on the town council. In Bushong, there's a woman, Louise Stillwell, who owns and operates her very own pharmacy, Still-well's Drugstore, and—"

He interrupted, "That's different." He waved his cigar before putting it back in his mouth. "Maretta is single and her shop is lady-like. Mules—for god-sake, are not. The grocer's wife is working *for* her husband. He's the boss, the owner of the store. That's why, I'm sure, that she's leaving her place on the city council. It's not ladylike and he needs her help at the store for feminine decisions." His know-it-all expression said that Mr. Noack owned his wife, as well.

"Elsa has done a wonderful job for the town the two years she's served on the city council. It will be a loss, actually. She's giving up the seat because she wants to be home more, as well as at the store." Jocelyn's glare caught fire from his smirk and she said pointedly, "It'll be hard to find the right person to replace her abilities on the council."

He bellowed a laugh. "I doubt that, dear lady." His chest puffed out in self-approval, dismissing her words with a deep grunt. "No, it will be easy. But back to you, Mrs. Pladson, your business—the livery stable—isn't fit for a decent woman like yourself to be tied to. I do pity you, Mrs. Pladson." He stroked his maroon silk tie into the exact place, first eyeing her, then the mules, and back to her. His manner as solemn as a minister at a funeral. "You're about to make yourself the laughing-stock of the county. Disrespected. The town of Skiddy's biggest embarrassment." He threw his shoulders back, his eyes cold, and concluded, "I'm surprised that your husband would allow you to do something so unbecoming."

And I suppose your rank musk cologne along with

the stink of your cigars—that is about to make me upchuck—is to cover the homey hay and horse smells of my livery?

Prank, who'd been waiting on a customer who wanted to buy horseshoes from the extra supply the livery kept, continually looked in her direction, his face tight with worry. She made a motion that she could handle this bloated goat, herself. Prank finished with the customer and went to forking hay to horses in their stall, while she continued to argue.

"It's clear, Mr. Cochran, that you know nothing about my husband, Pete. What he would or wouldn't 'allow'. Nothing. You talk as if I belong to him, his slave or whatever it is you think. He is not like that at all." *Pete is so different from you, a much better man than you could even dream of being. You, cruel in your greed, your gambling and cheating. Even worse in your attitude toward women. My husband, in every way, is the complete opposite of you and I thank Sweet Hannah for that!*

Facing up to him, she wanted to argue further, to tell him a thing or two about women's suffrage as she knew it, the rights they'd been denied for so long, how wrong it was. But he really wasn't worth her attention, and Prank was talking to him now, leaving off forking hay. The old man gripped the pitchfork, his eyes flashing anger. "I figger that you don't have any more business here today, Mr. Cochran. I reckon it's time for you to be goin' along."

Cochran looked surprised for a moment, sized up Prank's attitude and the ready pitchfork in his hands. He looked about to argue, then he waved a rude dismissal and turned, walking stiff-backed toward the livery's wide-open front doors to the street. He looked over his shoulder, his voice cold, "The loss with those half-dead mules you bought is yours, people, I'm glad the problem is not mine."

Prank muttered after him, "You'd be better off if you kept your mouth shet, Mister. And if you bother my boss again, I'll—I'll pure dee pitchfork you into chicken feed! You ain't hornswoggling nobody in this town, ya durn rascal." He jabbed the fork hard a couple times at Cochran's disappearing figure.

Jocelyn grimaced at the picture Prank's words made. A second or two later, a grin twitched at the corners of her mouth when Prank said sympathetically, "I run him off for you ma'am."

"Yes," she kept a straight face, "you surely did."

Andy had come to yank at her skirt. "Momma, can we go to Mr. George's feed place? See the baby chicks? Please, momma, please?" She smiled down on him, took an orange-cream stick candy from her pocket, unwrapped it and gave it to him. In all the muss and fuss she'd forgotten she had the candy for him. He grinned back at her. "Now we can see the chickies. Yes?"

She was tired and preferred to head for home, right now, but she gave in. "We can, Son, but only for a minute or two at Mr. Jacobsen's feed store. Come along." Andy hopped and skipped in high spirits as they headed into the street. Halfway over, he looked up with devilment in his eye, raised a booted foot to tromp through a pile of dried horse dung and she yanked him back. "You know better, Andy." She hid a grin, looked stern, and he sobered. They continued the next few blocks to the outskirts of town, Andy's legs lifting in a sharp march the last few yards to

JACOBSEN'S FEED And SEED STORE. Dealers Also In Poultry, Eggs, Small Farm Tools And More.

George, a straw-haired, long-limbed man in sage-colored shirt and trousers, was waiting on a customer in the feed section further back in the store, but Jocelyn and Andy had no trouble finding the large pen of chirping fuzzy yellow chicks. When George finished with the other customer, he came striding toward them with a wide grin, his soft brown eyes kindly. "Sure good to see you two. Bet the little fella would like to hold a chick, hmm?"

"He would, but I'm afraid he'd get the chick all sticky with orange candy. Next time, he will." She grew serious. "I hear that you're thinking of running for Elsa Noack's spot on the town council. Have you decided? I hope that you will."

"I'm considering it, yes." He adjusted his wire-rimmed spectacles, scratched at his thick, bowl-cut straw hair. "I care about this little town, and I don't like the message J.L. Cochran is spreading in every direction, that we have no use for a livery stable with motor-cars coming along. I suppose I'd be doing the town a favor, providing I ran and won—stopping at least part of his scheme to have your property for a motorcar busi-ness. I dunno, yet. I might run."

They continued to talk about the town, going over a few things that could use correction, and more so, small though Skiddy was, favored aspects like the hotel and its dining room, Noack's Mercantile, the railroad station —a favorable shipping point for cattle and wheat. The post office and many other pluses that made Skiddy the fine place that it was and that should never be lost.

"I think you'd win, George, with your qualifications. Skiddy folks like you, have respect for how you run your business and its importance, but it's up to you, of course."

"Thanks, Mrs. Pladson, I'll keep that in mind." He was looking at the noisy chicks, his attention suddenly seeming more on them.

"Well, the young'un and I'd better be heading home." She caught Andy's hand, pulling him away from the pen of chicks, breaking his spell of fascination. Not that they didn't have chicks at home on the ranch, she raised a batch or two every spring.

"Wait just a minute, I'll fix a little box of chicks so the boy can raise his own chickens."

"But we have—sure, go ahead, George, put them on our tab, then."

Five minutes later, Andy, a box of five chirping yellow chicks in his hands, looked up at George, his face solemn. "Thank you. Momma will want to fry them when they're growed, but I won't let her. They can make eggs, an' that's all."

"A good decision for a young farmer already." George kept a straight face and patted Andy on the head. "You take care, Mrs. Pladson, and howdy Pete for me."

Jocelyn smiled. "I will." Taking Andy's free hand, they left the feed store and walked back to the livery where Prank had the team and wagon ready for her. As was habit, she gave each of the mules a pat and soft words of appreciation. "You're a good mule, Alice. You, two, Zenith. Take us home now." She helped Andy up to his seat, climbed up after him, took the reins in one hand and released the brake with the other. "Bye, Prank," they waved at him, "and thank you." She heaved a deep sigh and briefly hugged Andy to her side. It had been a long, tiring day. In some ways good, but in other ways plumb off kilter.

"Hup mules, Alice, Zenith, get along there." She drove up to the hotel, set the brake, and waited for Nila to come out. Between the two of them, working fast, they should have supper on time. Being home was going to be heaven. For the short while it lasted. She had a feeling all hell was coming down, but surely that was her imagination.

SEVEN

J ocelyn stirred the flapjack batter a little more
fiercely than necessary. It had come blessed plain
with the passing days that she had no time to
concern herself with J.L.'s, and Maretta Rudd's,
continual ranting around town about the livery. No
time to worry what might be their next plan to put her
out of business. *None would be happening and they
might as well be sensible and give up.*

She pushed the hair out of her eyes with the back of
her hand and poured a round of batter into the sizzling
skillet. *Giving mind to my family, to chores on the ranch,
at the livery, and mule sales are far more important than
a couple of lunatics expecting to change everything
overnight.* She flipped the pancake.

The homey aroma of bubbling coffee filled the
kitchen while her mind chased all the things that took
time and were her responsibility—washing, ironing, and
mending clothes. Redding the house, making butter,
baking bread, cooking meals. She sighed, just thinking
of it. Milking the cow, feeding her chickens, gathering

eggs, tending the garden, keeping the woodbox full. Not that she had to do every bit of it alone. At this very moment Nila was getting Andy dressed for the day, singing a happy little song to him about green grass growing all around. Rom was out helping Pete with barn chores. She scooped up the pancake and added it to others in the warming oven.

Heavens how I love them, Jocelyn was thinking moments later, looking around at her family, now occupied with her flapjacks which they'd chosen to eat with gooseberry jam instead of maple syrup. When not waiting tables at the hotel, Nila was at home to care for Andy and do Jocelyn's chores, when she couldn't be there, along with her own. Rom helped out at the livery and alongside Pete on the ranch when especially needed. Her heart lifted further, reminded of the rare days they lazed back for a bit of jollification. *Like today,* her mind sang, while she passed the bacon, *we have a few deliciously free hours from toil and worry.* Rom and Pete's baseball game, and there'd be a picnic, too. Friends to visit with.

~

The day was picking up to be steaming hot in another hour and Jocelyn joined the group of women spreading quilts in the shade of clustered elm trees. Out in the field, men and boys talked things over and were about to begin the game. Jocelyn had barely sat down, Andy starting to play with other tots at the edge of the quilt brigade, when she spotted a familiar figure followed by two youngsters coming her way. *Tarsy Webber! She hardly ever saw her dear friend these busy days*. She stood up and hurried to meet her pretty, good-natured friend.

Coming closer, Jocelyn hesitated for half a second, taking note of the enormous cream-colored hat clustered with pink and purple violets, that Tarsy wore. The hat was one from Marretta's shop, she'd seen it in the window. *No matter*. She smiled and hurried to catch Tarsy's hands. "I'm so glad you've come, Tarsy. I don't see you nearly enough, my dear friend."

"I'm glad, too." She kissed Jocelyn's cheek. "Gordon wanted to watch Pete and Rom play baseball today, maybe join the game himself, and I was more than happy to bring the young'uns and come along."

"Very pretty dress, cotton lawn? Did you make it?" Jocelyn admired the white dress dotted with dainty blue posies, tiny tucks across the front, ruffles at the top of the long sleeves. Ankle length, of course.

"I did. Quite a job, but I'm pleased with the outcome." She turned to her children, lively son Jeremy, a few years older than Andy, and her curly-haired tot, Lucy. "Yes," she answered their plea, "you may play with the other children, just stay where I can see you."

"Pretty hat, too. Is it from Marretta's shop? I believe I saw it there."

"Thank you. Yes, it's one of Marretta's creations. The day I bought it, I went on to the livery to show it to you and hoped to have a short visit, but you weren't there that day. How are things with your new business?"

"I love owning the business but at the moment it's in the middle of a kerfuffle." She wiggled her eyebrows. "And one I've decided to shoo out of mind today. We'll talk about it another time. Let's sit down, the game is starting."

For the next half hour or so, the women were content to watch the game, Pete pitching and Rom catcher on their team, Gordon on second base. In short order, they had put the other team out and for a second time, Pete's team was up to bat. The sharp thwack of the bat against a ball had the women on their feet cheering, clapping hard when the base was reached. In unison they moaned in sympathy when the next batter on their team was tagged 'out'.

More than once the game slowed and women-talk resumed. Their chatter in tune with the chirping of birds in the trees above them. Some of the women went back to a small fancy piece of needlework—embroidery, crochet, or knitting, which in no way interfered with their bubbling conversations.

For the most part Jocelyn half listened to the others, her eyes glued to the game, watching her 'men' play. Enjoying right along with them the good time they were having. The day wore on and the game grew less exciting. It was then, from the corner of her eye, she caught a woman seated on a blanket some distance away, watching her. The woman in red and blue calico, stocky, darkly-tanned, and coarse looking, stared at Jocelyn with what appeared to be disapproval. Wondering what that was about, Jocelyn had looked around and made sure that Andy still played with a group of other tots a few feet away, not neglected. Nila, and Elise from the hat shop, stood chatting with other young women nearby.

Jocelyn checked her skirts, *yes, not a teensy bit of her ankles showed*. She'd worn her hair loose to her shoulders, tied with a wide red ribbon. *She supposed being barely thirty was too old for a girlish look, but Pete loved it. Was it something about her friend that she sat with, Tarsy Webber?* All she'd wanted was to relax and enjoy herself today and mostly, that was happening. The community picnic and ballgame were proving to be the perfect answer. *Was the woman finding fault with her, or what?* At that moment, the woman climbed to her feet and came striding her way.

"You're Mrs. Pladson, ain't you?" the woman barked, coming to stand in front of Jocelyn, blocking her view of the game. Rom had just smacked a ball hard, sending it sailing high toward another pasture.

Jocelyn ceased clapping, bit the inside of her cheek and looked up, managing to smile. "Yes, I am."

"The mule woman?" the woman plopped down beside Jocelyn, pushing her aside to make room on the blanket.

"Yes, I suppose you could call me that."

"The one who owns the livery stable in Skiddy?"

"The same. Ma'am, is there something wrong. Can I help you?"

"Nah, nothin' wrong. I like mules, my own self. Own a few. I just had to know if you was the Pladson woman I been hearin' about, seein' your signs, an' all. You don't look like a mule woman, 'way too pretty." The woman hesitated, her expression serious. "But say, if you ever wanna do some mule tradin', come look me up." She described the location of her ranch, not far north and east of Skiddy, got to her feet, shook her skirts into place. "Never thought I'd meet another mule woman." She grinned. "It's a pleasure." She held her rough, calloused hand for Jocelyn to shake. "My name's Ruthie Freeman. Come see me."

"Um, my pleasure, I'm glad we've met," Jocelyn said, standing. "I'm Jocelyn. This is my friend, Tarsy Webber. Maybe you've met?"

"Don't think so, not in person." Ruthie shook Tarsy's hand. "I think I may have seen you in Skiddy, Noack's store. Pretty hat."

"It's so nice to meet you. And thank you, I like my hat, too."

Ruthie looked around toward the group of men and boys coming slowly their way, laughing and talking up the game. "Game's over looks like. Better grab my young'un. Gotta get home to my man, he ain't feelin' pert right now." Seeing the other women's inquisitive expressions and murmurs of sympathy she explained. "Cow horned him, broke one or two ribs but he's gettin' lots better. Nice to meet you folks." She waved and loped toward a tall stringy boy who separated from the group and stopped to wait for her with a satisfied grin.

"If that don't beat all, I just met another 'mule woman'." Jocelyn shook her head in wonder.

"You did at that." Tarsy chuckled. "And she has mules for you. Who'd have thought you'd be doing business at a baseball game? Well, anyway, I think it was good luck for you, Jocelyn. Now I need to fetch my picnic basket and quilt from our wagon. Be back in a minute Jeremy, Lucy. You wait here, children, with Andy and his Momma."

Jocelyn headed for the Pladson wagon a few paces away, Andy and Tarsy's youngsters bouncing along behind. Nila and her friend Elise were already at the wagon lifting baskets out. In short order, food and utensils were readied on an extra quilt that had been covered with a tablecloth.

Pete and Rom, arms across one another's shoulders came up, sweat dripping, but both grinning widely. "We won!" Rom said, giving Nila's shoulder a brotherly shove.

"We saw." Nila shoved him back. "We saw it all, didn't we, Elise?' She looked at her sweet-faced friend with freckles and strawberry blonde hair. "Good game, Rom," she finally added.

Elise smiled shyly at Rom with adoration in her blue eyes. "You hit that ball plumb out of sight. Might not be found for years."

His face reddened and he shrugged, "Aww, maybe not that far." He gulped. "Sure fun, though, but so is rodeo and it's funner." He said suddenly to Pete, who was filling his plate, "Why was you callin' me 'Doc Bushong' Pete? Ain't Bushong a town down in Lyon County?" He tossed the ball into the air and caught it, then put it down and headed for the food. He liberally scooped beans, deviled eggs, watermelon pickles, fried chicken, and yeast rolls onto his crowded plate.

"Yep, Bushong is the name of the town. I'll tell you why I called you that, after we eat. Here, Nila," Pete said, when he saw she was pouring lemonade. "I'll have some of that."

Andy came and leaned into Jocelyn's skirts. "I'm hungry, Momma. Can I have my picnic now?"

"Sure enough, Son, you can. This is your plate I'm fixing. You sit over there by your daddy and I'll bring this to you right quick."

Other than an occasional clacking of spoon or fork

against plate, or a "this is so good" the meal passed in relative quiet.

Pete finished his third yeast roll slathered with plum butter, set aside his empty plate, laid back in the grass, crossed his legs at his ankles, and hands behind his head closed his eyes.

"You didn't tell me, Pete," Rom protested.

"Tell you what?" He raised his head, his sleepy expression puzzled.

"You didn't explain why you called me 'Doc Bushong'."

"Oh, yeah." Pete blinked at Rom. "Forgot." He sat up and Andy sprawled in his lap. "It's interesting. Y'all will like to hear this," he motioned to Jocelyn, Nila and Elise. They put away the rest of the dishes, and one by one dropped to sit on the quilt to listen, skirts tucked neatly around their ankles.

"Doc Bushong—his real name is Albert J. Bushong —is a dentist now, but when he was a young fella, he was a great baseball player. Catcher for the St. Louis Browns."

Rom's eyes widened and he sat up straighter from his place in the grass. He chomped a large bite of their last chicken drumstick, chewed, licked his lips, and waved the bone for Pete to continue.

Pete grinned. "At the time the Browns won the World Series in 1886, Albert Bushong had played every game in the series. Yep. He was at bat in game six, prob-ably drawing full attention of the pitcher, when another player scored by stealing home, making the winning run."

Rom grinned widely. "Good for ol' Bushong."

"Wait now, you wanna hear this. Winning that

World Series got the attention of the Missouri Pacific Railroad bigwigs. The town of Bushong, down near Emporia, was just a little whistle-stop on their line, named Weeks, then. The Missouri Pacific Railroad high muckamuck honored several St. Louis players by naming some of their depots after them." He shook his finger slowly toward his rapt audience. "The moral of this story is that the town of Bushong is still no more than a whistle stop, and may always be, but it got its proud name from one of history's greatest baseball catchers. Y'all remember that." Seeing doubt in some of their faces, Pete added, "It's fact. A railroad man told me all about it. Heard the same thing another time from a fella who grew up in Bushong."

Across the way, on the Webber quilt, their friend Gordon sang out, "It's true, Rom, boy, all true, everybody."

"I still don't know why you called me that, Pete, I ain't never played baseball much. Only had a couple good runs today."

"I was funnin' you, Rom. But you never know, Son, you never know."

"That's a great story, Pete," Jocelyn said, lifting a sleepy Andy from his lap and standing him on his feet. "It's been a good day any way you look at it. But now we need to be heading home and evening chores." She held Andy's hand and grabbed the picnic basket. Pete went to bring the team and wagon. Nila and Elise folded the quilts and Rom, with a mischievous grin, took the quilts to carry and gave Elise his mitt and baseball to hold.

Watching, Jocelyn felt a moment of delight, followed by a twinge of sadness and her steps slowed.

She'd expected to bear another child, after Andy, but it hadn't happened. He remained their miracle baby. And now these young folks had grown up so fast, would be taking off to follow their own dreams before long. They'd find somebody to love, marry, have their own home and family. She was going to miss Nila and Rom something terrible when that happened. Pete would, too. And she didn't want to think how much Andy would miss them. Whatever those two did, wherever they went, she hoped to Hannah that they'd visit now and then. Come home to see them. *I couldn't bear it any other way.*

EIGHT

To Jocelyn's satisfaction, word continued that she was buying mules, likely by word of mouth as well as from their flyers and signs. She made a few good buys of young healthy mules from Ruthie Freeman, the woman she'd met at the ballgame. Mules that could be trained to halter and could be sold as working teams. She was more than pleased with the two sickly mules she'd purchased from poor Mr. Ivers, the evicted farmer. With special treatment, first a rub down with coal oil as Prank had suggested then a salve from the vet, plus feeding them up, they were improving daily. In another few months to a year, they'd be saleable, for a greater price than she paid.

~

Leaving Andy at home with Nila, Jocelyn traveled alone half a day to the Riley ranch across the county line, south, through endless rolling land, a warm westerly wind making waves in the tall grass. Her spirits rose as she drove through the gate to the ranch. *With luck, she'd be buying several fine mules today.* Dust rose around her as she drew her mule team to a halt.

"Are you Mr. Riley?" she called to the man in a nearby corral, brushing down an already sleek bay horse. "I'm Mrs. Pladson, from the Skiddy Livery, here for a look at mules."

He left the corral, strode to stand by her wagon. "I'm Arthur Riley, owner of this ranch, but I'm afraid I have bad news for you."

"Bad news? They've all been bought?"

"Not that at all, sorry to say. Practically overnight my mule herd has been about wiped out by botulism poisoning, Mrs. Pladson." Wiping a hand down his face, he explained. "The first one or two that got sick and died, we thought had rabies, you know?" His hands flared. "That they'd been bit by some rabid dog, or coyote—not that that would have been any better an outcome. When more of my mule herd got sick showing the same blind staggers, we got a vet to look at them and he found the trouble was botulism. From bad water in the creek, or toxic feed—decaying hay, although I've not been able to trace it to either. Only one other option that I know of, that's in the soil, and I'm looking into that."

"Mr. Riley, I'm so sorry."

Breathing heavy, pain in his eyes, he told her, "Whole damn herd is about gone, the vet said there's no treatment. Don't expect you want to look at the few we got left?" His voice thickened, "Seeing as how they could come down with the disease any day, though they look fine right now?"

She hesitated, bit her lip, set the brake, tossed the reins aside and climbed from the wagon, following him to a pasture on the other side of the barn. *I'll look at his animals to be polite but I can't do this, I just can't.* Feeling guilty, she held her arms tight to her stomach.

For several minutes she stood at his side, looking at the grazing mules that did seem healthy enough, at the moment. She could chance it, but what if they died on her? Maybe she was imagining it, but she thought she could smell the stink of decay in the air, possibly from dead animals he'd buried. He was a good fellow, and she hated turning him down. She cleared her throat. "I'm sorry, Mr. Riley, truly I am, about what's happened to your herd. I'd like to help out, but I can't afford the risk." Disappointed after coming so far, and sick inside with sympathy, she attempted a smile of possibility. "I'll wait a while, maybe a month or two, and I'll come back and if the disease is clearly gone, we might be able to do business."

He backed away, his arms hanging at his sides in defeat. He walked with her to her wagon and team. "I'm not blaming you. Truth is, I was thinking about the same." He tipped his hat and with a gusty sigh turned toward the corral where the bay waited. He looked back at her. "Thank you, Mrs. Pladson. I hope to see you again under better circumstances. When that comes, I might be buying healthy mules off of you." He touched his hat again and pushed on through the corral gate.

Jocelyn watched the poor man take up with his horse again, thinking to herself as she climbed up onto the wagon bench, *I'm blessed tired and came all this way for nothing but that Riley fellow is a lot worse off than I am.* She shook the reins over the mules, her wagon rattling back toward home.

At the ranch, later, weary as she was, she answered yes to Pete's mention of attending a barn dance that night at the Webber's. She bathed, put on her prettiest outfit, an eight gored skirt in royal blue and a lace-trimmed white shirtwaist. She brushed her hair and fastened it in a twist on top of her head, leaving a soft curl on each side of her face. *It would be heaven to spend an evening dancing in Pete's arms. A late-night drive home in the moonlight, cuddled beside him, even better.*

A fter a morning spent buying supplies at Noack's mercantile, going over the livery's ledger and a discussion with Prank about their growing mule herd and the need to hold a sale, soon, Jocelyn stepped outside the stable barn and eyed the position of the sun. She went back in and pulled Andy away from climbing in and out the bottom rungs of the ladder to the loft. She said to Prank, "I think I'll have time on the way home to head up to that fellow, Ben Stewart's, ranch for a look at those mules he mentioned to you." The place sat practically on the Morris County, Geary County line and not far from Skiddy. "C'mon, Son, let's go." He ran ahead to the wagon.

"You met the Stewarts, ain't you?" Prank asked, coming up behind her.

"I've seen them a time or two. Don't know a lot about them, but I've heard that Mr. Stewart is a fine man, and has a good-sized ranch."

"An' that's the truth about Ben. You don't see his wife, hardly, I've heard things about the poor woman from some'a their neighbors who come here for business."

Jocelyn turned. "What've you heard? Is it important?"

He hesitated. "Some say that his Missus acts up strange is all, a trifle teched."

She shrugged, and smiled. "Maybe she's just shy." She motioned to Rom who'd been currying a horse and presently was putting up curry combs and brushes, and the cleaning rags he'd been using on the horse's hooves. "If you're coming home with me, Rom, better hop to it. We'll be taking a side trip to look at some mules on the way. We need to go now. The sun won't wait for us to reach home before it goes down."

"Fine," he called, "but let me drive. You wanta' be home before dark, I'll see to it." He trotted past her, gave her a wide teasing grin, and hopped into place on the wagon. He tousled Andy's hair and picked up the reins.

"Smart thing," Jocelyn replied, climbing up settling onto her end of the seat, "don't think for a minute you're going to run these mules into the ground. I won't have it." She did her best to look stern, with little luck.

A short while later they came to a lane leading off from the side of the road. Jocelyn motioned for Rom to turn that way. At the end of it, in the distance, was a small house and clustered ranch buildings.

"This is the place, sure enough, Rom." With a half-smile, Jocelyn eyed the grey weathered barn and its stone foundation as they approached. The barn a centerpiece to other outbuildings, pens, a garden and a small white house. On every side as far one could see, horses and mules grazed belly-high pastures. More tall-grass pastures, waving in the wind, were speckled here and there with grazing cattle. She read aloud the enormous sign fading on the side of the barn, "*CHEW MAIL POUCH TOBACCO, Treat Yourself to the Best.*"

Rom chuckled. "I gotta try that chew some time. Must taste like apple pie."

"It can't! You see them spit it out, don't you? Well, then, that means something."

"The way I see old gents out front of the barbershop in Skiddy, jaws stuffed and chawin', it might taste mighty fine for a while, Ma."

"Shush your joking. I doubt that very much, and here comes a man from the barn, likely the rancher who has the mule colts for sale." She looked over her shoulder, made sure that Andy still slept on the horse blanket in the wagon bed. Poor tot. Sometimes she wondered if dragging him hither and yon was a good idea. She climbed from the wagon. A lanky, pleasant-faced man in typical ranchman's garb, dusty and faded, approached. She smiled. "Hello. Mr. Stewart? You have a few mules for sale, I believe?"

He tipped his weather-worn, wide-brimmed hat to her. "I do. You're Mrs. Pladson? I've been told you wanted a look at my herd."

"Yes, I'm Mrs. Pladson. This is Rom, my son. Back there asleep is my little boy, Andy."

He shook Rom's hand, and thumbed behind him. "My son, Lafe, is bringing the mules to the corral yonder. Come on an' look 'em over." He set off, leading the way.

A half dozen mule colts and mule fillies—sorrels,

bays, and one white, churned into the corral, raising dust. Some turned toward the humans, ears perked with interest, others flopped down to roll in the dust. They were such fetching creatures they made Jocelyn laugh.

Rom, who cared for their mule team, Alice and Zenith, and who practically lived with the mule colt, Shay, considered himself as good a judge of mules as anybody. He was over the corral fence and giving Stewart's mules closer looks. Jocelyn followed through the gate Mr. Stewart held open for her. Like what Rom was already doing, she looked for what was called a "kind" eye in the mules, clear and healthy, and showing a calmness when she approached, making no effort to move away from her. She reached out and handled their ears, petting, because the mule's allowing that was so important to putting on bridles, halters, or rope. Would they put up with her touch all over? She stroked their neck, their back, even the tender spots inside the hind legs, the ears, and tail head. For the most part they allowed it. Occasionally they brayed, "e-e-e-onk, e-e-e-onk, onk, onk," seeming almost like conversation.

"Could we please see them in a trot?" Jocelyn requested. Ben Stewart nodded to his son, a young cowboy probably in his early twenties, astride a tall grey mule. One by one, Lafe Stewart roped a mule and led it at the run past Jocelyn and Rom, who watched carefully for any signs of lameness or pulling back on the rope in an effort to run away.

Several minutes later, the young mules were led away and reunited with their mommas. Jocelyn had picked three mule colts that she liked a lot. She pointed them out to Mr. Stewart, two chestnut bay male colts and the white filly mule. She asked, "Is there a chance I could buy them in pairs with their Mommas?" Buying individuals normally costs more than each in a pair together. When the time came, she could sell them individually and earn more than she paid for the pairs.

Mr. Stewart frowned. "I don't know if I can do that." He sighed. "Well, I do need to cut down on my herds. I reckon that I can sell you the roan mare with her bay colt, the buckskin mare with the other bay. Umm, and the sorrel mare with her white colt, for—oh, I'm cheating myself but how about a hundred dollars a pair?"

She shook her head. "That's more than I can pay, I'm sorry," She studied his face, waiting for him to change his mind and come down in price.

Minutes ticked by as they dickered back and forth. Mr. Stewart nodded and opened his mouth to speak just as a woman's scream sounded behind them.

Jocelyn whirled about. A woman, pretty but with tangled blonde hair, wearing one shoe, the other foot bare, and her apron wrong side out, charged toward them.

The rancher strode toward her, "Now, Bethie, what's got you so upset? You're supposed to be taking a nap." His voice was soft and kind. "Go on back to the house, dear, and I'll come, in a minute or two. We're about finished here, anyhow."

"She's the one, ain't she?" Clawed hands reaching, the woman charged at Jocelyn. "The one you been sportin' with when you go to town!"

Jocelyn stepped out of her reach, astonished. She attempted a smile, held her hand out in greeting. "I'm Mrs. Pladson. I..."

"No, you're not! You're the woman he's seein', evil

as sin." She charged at Jocelyn again, Mr. Stewart catching her struggling body in his arms just in time.

"I haven't been seeing anyone but you," Mr. Stewart protested. "You're my sweet wife and I love you. Now, let's get you back inside." He held the flailing woman close in his arms, looked at Jocelyn in apology, tears in his eyes for his poor loved one. "I'm sorry."

"You been keepin' company with this here witch on the sly, I know you have." The shrieking and bold kicking continued. Over in the wagon, Andy was awake and beginning to cry. Stewart's wife tore from her husband's arms and hurtled toward Andy in the wagon. "That's your child with her, you've even had a bastard child with her, I know you have."

"No, sweetheart, no, that's not true." He ran to catch up as she headed toward the wagon, Jocelyn fast on his heels. Someone had to stop this poor woman, now, and try to make good sense to her.

Like something wild, the wife shoved Jocelyn to the ground hard, ran to the wagon and snatched Andy into her arms, running toward the house with him as he sobbed, arms reaching back for Jocelyn. Gasping for the breath that had been knocked from her, Jocelyn climbed to her feet and panted, "It's all right, Son, Momma's coming. You'll be fine, don't cry." The woman holding him stopped. Eyes on her son, Jocelyn, slowly, carefully, took steps closer.

In a flash, the woman changed direction toward the well. *To throw him in?* "Put him down, put my son down, please." The woman hesitated, almost as though she had a moment of clarity, understanding the wrong she was about to do. She moved again, hurrying toward the well, Jocelyn close behind. "I love my son, please give him to me. I won't hurt you, but you must give me my baby."

Lafe Stewart shouted, "Ma, behave. Give the lady her child."

Rom, who at first had frozen in shock, hurried to Jocelyn's side. He warned, "Don't hurt my little brother. His momma wants him." He moved fast and grabbed Andy from the woman's arms just as she lifted him over the well. Rom almost threw him back to Jocelyn. She took her small son and ran. Gratitude in every vein, she looked back over her shoulder and stopped in her tracks, frightened for her older boy.

The woman grappled with Rom, hitting him in the face, in his throat, with her fist, kicking and trying to shove him aside. She turned on her husband when he tried to hold her to him, pounding him over and over. She sobbed, "He's mine, the little boy is mine. I want him for me."

Mr. Stewart held her close and called to Jocelyn who was now joined by Rom. "You and your boys need to go, Mrs. Pladson. Go, please. I'll bring the mules to you, and herd them to Skiddy."

His wife kicked furiously and screamed, "You ain't givin' your sportin' woman our mules. You ain't!"

"I'm not giving them to her," he told his wife gently, brushing the tangles of hair from her eyes. "I never met Mrs. Pladson 'til today and she is paying us well for the mules. Then we can get you to a special doctor in Topeka. He'll help you to not be so mixed up, honey." He turned her toward the house, nodding to Jocelyn and Rom over his shoulder to go.

Tears of sympathy welled in Jocelyn's eyes for the couple, blinding her. Once in their wagon, she mopped her eyes. Shaken to her core as they drove toward home, she chastised herself for exposing her small son, and Rom, even though a young man, to such a sad and worrisome situation. It was part of life, she had to admit, and a body never knew when or where something so painful would show. If at all possible, she was paying that poor fellow the price he asked, no more discussion, and should the stars be aligned right, that poor wife of his would be helped, made well again.

NINE

A week later, Jocelyn, standing at the livery's corral gate, hands pressed in a steeple to her lips, watched Mr. Stewart and his son, Lafe, depart for home. Their mounts fed, watered and rested, and her payment in Ben Stewart's vest pocket for the mare and young mule pairs they'd delivered. She'd invited the two men to join her for a noon meal but, understandably, Stewart was in a hurry to get home to his Beth, having left her in the care of Lafe's young wife. Now that he had the money, Ben Stewart would take his wife to see the doctor in Topeka.

Feeling good about the deal she made with Mr. Stewart, she headed to the livery stable to talk to Prank. She'd arrived in town from the ranch about the same time as the Stewarts reached the livery with her new mules and, whatever Prank, looking very upset, had been about to tell her, it had had to wait. She went to stand beside him where he shoveled manure into a wheelbarrow. "You had something on your mind to tell me earlier, Prank. What is it, you looked real bothered?"

His eyes flashed with anger, he dropped the shovel and spat over his shoulder. "Dad-blame his hide, that high-steppin' scalawag, J.L. Cockroach, come here like he owned the place, showin' a citified fella from somere's out of town around the livery barn, an' the pastures, everythin'." He hesitated, making odd noises in his throat. A look of sympathy joined his outrage. "Overheard him sayin' to the city fella that he had you practically talked into sellin' out. That a motorcar business could be built here soon as the fella' wanted."

She did a double-take. "That's impossible, Prank, you know it, too. Why would he lie like that? I'm not selling to J.L. or his friends, to anyone. Not for years. This is silly." She walked away a few paces and came back. "He might think I can be pushed out, shamed and badgered into dropping plans to keep the livery, but he's wrong, Prank, so wrong. I wouldn't quit if he held a gun to my head."

Prank faced her, his arms sweeping the air, worry wrinkling his forehead. "Cockroach strutted aroun' here like General Robert E. Lee sendin' his Rebels to take over Missouri! He told the other fella that he had ways to convince you, make you happy to sell all this at a dirt-cheap price. An' then they laughed at that. Made me mad as hell—pardon my cussin', Missus—the way they were talkin'. I pert-near clobbered Cockroach with the full basket of grain I was holdin'. Ordered them off the property. Told 'em the livery was yours and you'd be keepin' it a'runnin' a good long while, as needed. When they paid me no mind, I made out real serious that I was goin' to my office for my shotgun. And, dad blast it, I woulda'." He scratched his whiskery jaw. "That discouraged them 'nuff they left, but Cockroach said he'd be back. Told me I oughtta hit the road lookin' for another job 'cause I wasn't havin' this one long. Pshaw," he growled, shaking his head.

She was so furious it was hard to stay calm. "You don't have to listen to that nonsense, Prank. Your job is safe with me, for as long as you want."

"Made me maddern six shades of hell. By the way, the marshal came by right after those ratbags left and I tol' him everythin'. He said he wanted to talk to you about Cockroach's harrassin'. That a good woman like you don't deserve that kinda' treatment."

"Suits me. I've already wanted to talk to Marshal Hillis. I might as well do it today, after I go over the books for you."

"Fine and dandy." He turned to take care of a blue roan horse a cowboy had just led into the livery, turning to wave at another customer who'd taken time to brush and water his buckskin, had paid up, and was leaving.

Two hours later Jocelyn was in Marshal Hillis's office, sitting forward in her chair, her feet tapping and her mouth drying as she listened to him relate goings-on she'd not heard about until this minute.

"Cochran's out to finish you, that's for sure." He sat back in his chair, hands locked in front of his chest, his expression serious. "Him, with the help of that lady who has the hat shop. For days now, he's swaggered about, giving folks the glad-hand, letting them know about the big celebration he's putting on for the Fourth of July."

"Fourth of July celebration, him?"

"Yep. The money for it, or so he says, is coming from his own pocket. He's promising fireworks, games, decorations all around town. A pig roast, races, and other means of celebration, all from the kindness of his heart. He makes sure they know about that. His big-hearted kindness."

"I don't understand why he'd do this, greedy as he is. And a liar to boot. What for?"

"Greed is involved in a big way, I'm afraid. Truth is, he's trying to soften folks up, so they'll see his side, the why of his aim to get rid of the livery."

"How, in the name of Hannah, can a celebration do that?"

"If he can get the proposition to get rid of the livery on the upcoming city ballot, he believes folks'll be thinking highly enough of him and his plans to vote your business out. Kaput. Replace the livery with a motorcar dealership because any time now every person he blathers to, will want their own motorcar in the worst way. An' he'll be ready, with the best motorcars available." He cocked his head, his eyebrows rising. "The other side of that, folks are hungry for entertainment, Jocelyn. A full days' good time away from their everyday hard work, their tough lives. Sorry to say, from what I'm hearing, a number of folks may thank him with a vote his way."

"Dear heaven, I can't believe it." She clenched her jaw, her legs feeling twitchy as she stood up from her chair. *Thank heaven women could now vote in city affairs. Women would certainly have better sense than to vote J.L. for anything.* "I need to go to the mercantile for groceries, then home to the family. Thank you,

Marshal, for letting me know all this. I can at least be prepared."

He stood and escorted her to the door. "Try not to worry too much, Mrs. Pladson, I'm doing what I can. I'd like for you to keep this quiet for now, but I'm investigating him for underhanded doings he appears to be guilty of in the last town he came from and places before that. Actions that he's already into here in Skiddy."

"Just what, besides bedeviling me no-end about my operating the livery?" She fingered the ribbon tied at her neck, her jaws clamped while she waited.

"Well, for one example, going out of his way to make good friends with the local banker. Finding out ahead of time about possible foreclosures on someone's business, farm, or ranch, then buying them out cheap. Leaving some folks at rock bottom, near destitute, while he gets ahead."

She told him about the Ivers family she'd bought the sickly mules from. "J.L. all but stole that farm. Putting them out with next to nothing to live on, or a place to go."

"I knew about that. It was a sad affair. Some church folks did get together with donations of food and clothes and a few dollars to help the Ivers on their way west."

Hand clasped over her mouth, she was silent a moment, then asked. "What else can we do about J.L. Cochran? I wish we could run him out of town, permanently."

"That might could come one of these days. When his presence became less than tolerable in the last town where he had a business or two, he took off, for parts unknown at the time. Left the bank to take back what he considered 'owned' by him. Somehow, he borrowed money elsewhere, then invaded Skiddy to do the same things he's always done, here. Reminds me of some of the early homesteaders, the dishonest ones. They'd use the land they got free to homestead on as a surety, borrow from the bank for farm equipment, then light out with the cash. Only this time it's Cochran and an automobile business in the picture, added to the rest of his outlawry. He's getting closer to seeing himself behind bars." He scratched his nose, "Hell if he ain't, the fool."

She nodded. "I don't see how we can put up with him, at all. I know I'd like to see him gone, Marshal. Thanks again. You have given me hope."

At the mercantile, she heard much of the same information about the coming Fourth of July celebration from Mrs. Noack. "I'm skeptical about his getting the vote," she wiped down the glass cheese case with a wet cloth, "but it's hard to say." She gave a hesitant nod. "Quite a few folks who've come in here to the store acted excited about the celebration, and from all accounts their opinion of J.L. Cochran appears tending to rise."

"For the sake of Hannah, I hope this doesn't happen. That there's a way for it to be scotched."

～

When Jocelyn mentioned the Fourth of July Celebration at the supper table that night, Nila said, "I'd heard about the big doings for the Fourth, it sounds fun—if you can put out of mind who is behind it all."

Jocelyn tensed. With her hand wobbling, she set her iced tea glass back down on the table.

"I heard about it, too," Rom said. "I've heard that the old Cockroach is adding a rodeo to the doings. I can't wait to sign up for the competitions. Some say there's going to be a mule race, and I'm full on for that, too."

Jocelyn looked at her family, shocked, and elbows on the table, held her head in her hands.

Pete pulled one of her hands away, and leaned to kiss her cheek. "It's going to be fine, love. Everything's going to be Jim dandy."

She sniffed back tears of fury at J.L. and his intentions. "I suppose. I guess. Maybe it will." She got to her feet, and went to bring Nila's delectable looking pie to the table. "Thanks for baking the apple pie today—it looks so good, Nila. And even bigger thanks for taking care of Andy. You're so good with him." Her chin lifted as she sat back down.

I love these people around my table beyond any imaginable measure. They make the worst times, not so bad. Every time.

When everyone was busily eating their pie, Jocelyn, dry eyed, and coming to a sudden decision that excited her, said, "I know what I'm going to do to outfox that reprobate, J.L. Cochran." They all turned to look at her. She smiled. "I'll need every one of you to help."

"How's that, Jocelyn?" Nila asked, "What's your plan?" She waited, wearing an eager expression.

"I'll do a smart of thinking more about it and then I'll let you all know." Pete and Nila groaned a bit, but she didn't budge. They'd know, soon.

"J.L. Cochran's Fourth of July picnic is pure bribery for votes. There should be a law against it," Jocelyn told Mabel Goody, who'd stopped by for a visit and had taken a chair across from her at the kitchen table. She pushed the sugar bowl to Mable and took a sip of iced tea.

"You can't stop the celebration that he's holding, dear." Mabel added three heaping teaspoonfuls of sugar to her tea, stirring with a vigorous clinking. "There's been a passel of preparations made already and a lot of folks are counting on a good time at Cochran's big doings. There'd be a fury against you if you even tried to put a pox on it."

"I know." Jocelyn leaned toward Mabel and placed her hand flat on the table. "I don't intend to stop the picnic, the celebration, Mabel, nothing of the sort. I'm going to take advantage of it." In answer to Mabel's deep squint and dropped mouth, she said, "I expect folks from every direction will be coming to town to have a good time. Skiddy will be crowded one end of town to the other." She hesitated, gave Mabel a level look. "I'm going to have my first sizable mule sale that day, too. Make personal use of Cochran's crowd, to help save my livery. That's just the beginning. There are more ways than one to skin a skunk."

Mabel sat back and laughed. "That's a plumb good idea, Jocelyn." She sobered after a minute. "But won't he think that you're selling your mules, selling out because you're giving up?"

"I don't care what he thinks, he'll be wrong." There was an edge to her chuckle. "I won't be selling just my mules, I'll be inviting folks to bring their extra mules and horses to be sold with mine, or traded, too. I intend to provide an ample lunch, plenty of places for folks to sit and visit, talk business." She hesitated for a second or two. "Some of them will make money selling, others will be buying mules that they've been wanting. I mean to show that the Skiddy Livery is a growing, busy, blessed well needed business. Not, by anybody's high dudgeon, is it going to be destroyed and replaced." *Dudgeon, if I remember the word correctly from childhood reading, meant angry if one isn't getting their way.*

"I declare, dear woman, you got a head on your shoulders and there's a good chance you'll beat that rascal at his own game."

"That's the plan," Jocelyn said quietly, chin up, "that's the plan."

Mabel tapped her fingers on the table, excitement in her voice, "Sausages with buns to hold 'em, peach and cherry hand pies, popped corn, lemonade and iced tea. Let me take over the food part of your plan, Jocelyn, I want to help." She nodded agreement to her own suggestion. "I'll get some of our women-friends to make and serve the fixin's. I know that Tarsy Webber will agree to lend a hand, and Emma Hunter. Maggie Rowland will want to, and some others."

"Would you, Mabel? Nobody could do that better than you, with our good friends. It'd be such a help."

"'Course we will. Our men folks'll be glad to help Pete and Rom handle the stock for the sale, too. Now I think on it, Lyman has been wantin' to put our old mule, Jolly Bird, out to pasture and buy himself a younger and stouter one, or two."

"Y'all are the kindest sort of neighbors."

"No more than you and Pete, you'd do the same for us. Besides, keepin' that livery business is as important to us as customers as it is to you as owner. The Skiddy Livery has to stay."

"It does, and now to get to work." They smiled at one another, took a last gulp of tea—Jocelyn making a face because hers was too sugary at the bottom—and pushed back from the table.

Two days later, from morning to late afternoon, small herds of mules were hazed into town, leaving clouds of dust hanging in the air as they headed to the fenced pastures behind the livery. Jocelyn and her helpers were here, there, and everywhere, aiding folks—both sellers and buyers, setting up their tents, finding spots for their wagons and campfires. There were few times in her life that Jocelyn had been so excited. As the day wore on toward evening and a setting sun, conversations, happy shouts, and guitar strumming swirled around her. Delicious smells of frying potatoes and meat had her close to swooning.

Andy had had the time of his life all afternoon, visiting camp spot to camp spot where he was fussed over and given treats—a slice of apple, a twist of taffy, an ear of buttered sweet corn—from her women friends and other folks she'd met through mule sales. So many folks in town today. What was J.L. Cochran up to right now? she wondered. *No way on earth could he, would he, be able to best me. No sir, not the way my plans are becoming fact.* She momentarily chastised herself for such braggerly thoughts, but in the back of her mind she meant them anyway. Breaking the moment of a sudden, was the smell of cigar smoke close behind her. She spun around.

TEN

J.L. Cochran chewed his cigar, puffing ferociously. "What the hell is going on here? Looks like a damn circus. You trying to draw folks away from my celebration from over by the hotel? I planned this day, not you. It's my party for folks, not yours." Raising his arm, cigar in hand, he waved a wide loop which all but said, *my town, any day now I'll own it.*

"I understand what you're saying, J.L., but Independence Day has belonged to everyone—from the moment it was declared in 1776." Her voice cooled. "The folks here are just having a good time, taking part in your celebration, and mine. That's reasonable, isn't it? We, the livery, is a Skiddy business, we're not outsiders to the town, we belong. I didn't realize that you'd mind." She licked her lips and despite feeling a trifle shaky, she pasted on an innocent smile.

Anger flared in his face. "Why are all those wagon camps back there? Those mules? Is all this going on because you're selling out, or not? I gotta know which it is here and now, dammit." He sucked on his pipe.

"Isn't that what you wanted?" Glaring at him in self-defense was no problem. "I thought it was." *Though it isn't a trifle of your business whether I stay until all eternity, or pack up tomorrow.*

Sudden loud sobbing close by had both of them turning. Mabel stumbled up to them, wailing and mopping her face, "It just ain't going to be the same not having you here, Jocelyn. It just breaks my heart you got no choice but to leave." Her eyes privately told Jocelyn a different story.

That Mabel, making out that my mule sale is the end! Playacting that I'm giving up. Bless her heart, though her act might not be taken as actual by J.L., cursed pesky man. Jocelyn stood her ground, straining to hold back the laugh that threatened to bubble from inside her—and continued her hard look at Cochran, her mouth pinched and her backbone stiff as iron.

"All the downtown folks are going to miss you, Jocelyn." Elsa from the mercantile joined them, dabbing delicately at her eyes with a handkerchief, appearing to make an effort to control herself. "We've really liked having you among us Skiddy business owners. We expected you to be here in town, dear, for a long time yet. Years. But life is what it is, the good and the bad." She sniffled, blew her nose into her handkerchief, wiped her nose and glared in J.L.'s direction.

Tarsy Webber was next, then Maggie Rowland, Emma Hunter, one after another—a whole passel of women-friends clustered around Jocelyn, all teary-eyed over the misfortune of her faked leaving.

"What the hell, what the damn hell?" J.L. mumbled, chewing his cigar and backing away from the circle of women.

Hands on her hips, defiance burning in her throat, Jocelyn swiped at her actually dry eyes and asked, "Haven't you seen enough, done enough? Get on back to your own celebration and leave us alone in our misery you've caused. I have enough to do before I go." *Home tonight*.

Satisfaction eased through Jocelyn as she watched him stomp off in the direction of his celebration, looking back over his shoulder once or twice, doubtful, angry. Her friends continued their pretense of crying, quite loudly now, clustering close to her, until J.L. was long out of sight.

"Now then," Mabel Goody grinned, "wasn't you glad to see us weepers come to your aid?"

"Do you think he swallowed our actin'?" red-haired Maggie Rowland wondered, "or did we just scare him off? I s'pose it don't matter which."

Emma Hunter put her arms around Jocelyn. "We women would hate like tunket if that man ruined your livery. We did help you, didn't we, with our little performance? Truth to tell, I thought we put Shakespeare to shame."

Jocelyn gasped from laughing so much, wiped tears from her cheeks with the heel of her hand. "Y'all did help and I can't tell you how much. Whether he believes I'm actually leaving, and today was a last good-bye, or not, I thank you all." Her knees no longer felt wobbly from facing down Cochran. "The sun is about to go down, about time we put things to rights and make ready to go—home, so's to be ready for tomorrow, the big day." Parting, they shot sneaky smiles at one another.

Next day at home on the ranch, a satchel of necessary papers and other needs for the day in hand, Jocelyn hurried through the dark to the wagon where Pete, Andy, and Nila waited. Anxious to be at their mule sale today, and much to do, they had completed chores on the ranch long before dawn broke. Rom had already left, riding his mule, Shay. He was somewhat out of sorts that the rodeo set for today had been canceled. Rumor had it that local ranchers weren't interested in siding with Cochran and refused to provide riding stock, their riders in agreement.

"I wish we could have spent the night in Skiddy and then we'd already be there," Jocelyn told Pete as they drove along. "I'm glad we got chores done decently at home, though."

He patted her knee but remained silent.

She continued, "J.L. Cochran fumed about the goings on at our livery yesterday." She went on to tell him the whole story, unable to keep a straight face. "I found out later that he got the idea earlier, from someone—I don't know who—that we really would be selling out today. That story spread, probably with help from our friends, until, they say, he was plumb jubilant that I was letting him have his way. Nobody was telling him different far as I know."

A short silence followed. Jocelyn tipped her head back, eyes closed. "It might've been Ruthie Freeman, the other 'mule woman' who I met at the ball game, that started the story saying I was finished and selling out. She was the first to arrive, with her helper and the mules they wanted to sell. She's become a good friend and I was so glad to see her." She turned to face Pete as the wagon bumped along in the half dark. "Art Riley came to look and to buy, losing so much of his herd how he did to that pestilence, and Ben Stewart, like some others, says he's come to do both, buy and sell." She finished worriedly, "J.L. is a fool, and I'm guessing he doesn't know women's ways much. Even so, he might've caught on by now that my friends were pretending, trying to make him a fool. That I wasn't going anywhere but home for the night, the livery staying like an ancient rock."

"He likely knew you were tryin' to trick him, hon, and he just needed time to figure out how to get even." He looked down at her, his eyes filled with concern. "You stay clear of that man, Jocey. He's got a streak of the devil in him and he's going to be mad as hornets in hades if he knows for sure that you women made a fool of him. Who knows what he'll do to even the score? I sure as hell don't have any idea, but I'll have my eye out for him. You take care, too."

"I'll be too busy to even know he's around, Pete, and he'll be the one taking care, wanting to impress people how he intends." Her palms had become sweaty, but she was blessed if she'd give in to fear of the reprobate.

Too late, Jocelyn realized that Andy and Nila, right behind them in the wagon, had heard their discussion. Nila, who was wearing a pretty straw hat trimmed with pink velvet roses and a snowy white egret feather, that a customer at the hotel had given her, said, "If J.L. is even rude to you, Ma, I'll make him sorry with my hatpin." She showed it, eight inches long with a green bead top, a menace to anybody.

Jocelyn drew a deep breath in surprise. *Wouldn't it be right comical if...no, I shouldn't think that way.*

"I'll do this." Andy stood up in the wagon, fists flailing like a windmill. "I won't let Mr. Jail hurt you, Momma."

Jocelyn covered her mouth, smothering a laugh. *'Mr. Jail', indeed.* She turned, raising her eyebrow at Nila and reaching to catch Andy's hand. "There's nothing for you two to worry about, honestly. I'll be fine." *In time, 'Mr. Jail' would be in jail where J.L. should be.*

The sun was just turning a rose and yellow splash on the eastern horizon when they reached Skiddy, driving slowly along main street. Already more people than usual were up and about on the sidewalks, stopping to talk in pairs, heading into Noack's mercantile, or tying their horse or team to the hitchrail in the cool of morning.

As they drew in at the livery, Jocelyn smiled, noting out in the back pastures small groups of folks chatting, coffee cups in hand, the smells of smoke, frying bacon and pancakes in the air. Mules brayed, horses nickered —music to Jocelyn's ears.

Nila lifted Andy from the wagon. "C'mon, little brother, we're having a lot of fun today, you and me." She told Jocelyn, "I can keep watch on Andy, and give you a hand, too."

Jocelyn waved them off. "Nah, take him for a walk, he'll enjoy the sights. You enjoy yourself, too, Nila. I'll have plenty of help. I'm going to visit with a friend or two in the livery yard, before we get too busy." Prank had come to talk to Pete, who was unhitching their mule team. In short order, Alice and Zenith ambled toward the water trough, snatching a mouthful or two of grass as they went. Seeing everything under control, Jocelyn made her way back toward the campers. Busy as she was yesterday, she hadn't had time for a conversation with Ben Stewart and, seeing him in the midst of the mules he'd brought to sell, she turned his way now. He saw her coming, walked to meet her, nodded and smiled.

"Good morning, Mrs. Pladson. Quite a show you have going on here."

"Isn't that the truth. I've been wanting to ask about your wife. How's Beth? I've been so worried about her, about both of you. I'm so sorry we upset her that day at your farm."

He stroked an eyebrow, his smile fading a bit. "She's in the hands of good folks, being treated in a hospital in Topeka." His chin lifted. "The doctor tells me Beth shows signs of getting better. That's something we didn't have before, her calming down, reacting to folks with reason."

"That is good news."

"Yep. We, my boy, Lafe, and me, visit her and it's plain she likes to see us. I dunno." His voice cracked, "The doctor says there is a good chance she'll get well in her mind, be herself again. I just want her home."

Jocelyn's throat filled and she touched his arm. "It'll happen, Ben. I can't help but believe that she'll be fine and home with you again soon. Please, if there is anything I, or my husband, Pete, can do for you, let us know. Will you, Ben?"

His face broke into a tired smile. "You're already helping me, fixin' so I can sell my mules here today."

"It's our pleasure and I hope you get deals more than fair!"

"I'd like to see that myself." His expression brightened further. "If that's goin' to happen, I better get back to my mules. I'm brushin' 'em all 'til they shine. Did some hoof and mane trimmin' before we came."

"We did, too—well, my menfolk took care of most of it."

"As ought to be." He gave a short wave and turned away.

At that moment, she saw Lyman and Mabel Goody pulling up in their buggy and went to meet them. For the next hour, she helped Mabel unload food supplies—dish-toweled bundles of wonderfully fragrant yeast buns, brown paper wrapped stacks of sausages, huge bowls of apples, doughnuts and more—arranging them on the tented tables that had been set up the day before. Doing the same with other women friends as they arrived. Sounds of excitement surrounded them, happy chatter, laughter and teasing shouts. An occasional whinny from a horse in the corral, an *eee-onk onk onk* echoed by a mule or two, and adding to the chorus, down the street the barking of a dog.

"Well, Mrs. Pladson, I went and done it." Jocelyn recognized George Jacobsen's voice coming from her right.

She turned. "Hello, George. You did what?"

"I gave in and agreed to run for the vacant seat on the town council. My name'll be on the ballot." He leaned back, hands in his vest pockets, his eyes waiting for her reaction.

"You did? I'm so glad." She shook his hand, more than pleased with his decision. "Congratulations,

George, this is excellent news. You'll do a dandy job on the council, I know."

"Maybe up to scratch, anyway." His grin deepened. "Dependin' if I win, first. Where's Pete at? I came to help him and the other fellas. Figurin' that doin' my part today will earn me some votes later."

She smiled. "You'd have had them anyway." She motioned toward the hay barn. "Pete, Rom and Prank are over there finishing up moving everything aside not needed at this time, and placing a buckboard with the sides off as platform for the auctioneer. Some other fellas are fixing a fenced arena in the center of the barn for showing the stock animals up for sale. Seating will be a little sketchy, benches have been gathered for those who'd be bothered to stand. If it turns out to be an over-flow crowd, I expect some will find a seat on the rental buggies pushed over to the walls."

He tipped his hat to her. "It'll likely be all done before I get over there. Reckon that I'll sign on to help with the stock, or whatever else Pete needs me for. Gotta earn those votes." He hurried away.

"Thanks, George!" She called after him, *and praise be that you're running for town council, at least one much-needed roadblock against Cochran and his fool plans.*

By ten o'clock, the temperature had become hot and steamy. Thankfully, preparations for the day were near complete. Out front of the livery, shielding her eyes from the glare of morning sunshine, Jocelyn took a look down the street, watched a flag go up out front of the hotel, and chairs placed on the hotel porch for the mayor and other dignitaries who'd be making Independence Day speeches. She stood watching, taking it all in and feeling the building excitement as more and more people arrived. Dust coils followed horse or mule-drawn buggies. The same with wagons creaking and rattling along, many loaded with waving, laughing children. Riders on horseback clip-clopped in one direction, some the other way. Dust hung in the air while the comers filled hitch rails on both sides of the street.

Jocelyn was particularly pleased that so many folks headed directly to where she stood just outside the livery's wide doors, stopping to tell her hello and shake her hand before heading on to the hay barn and the sale about to commence. Her mouth dried from thanking one person after another and sharing in brief conversation, her face grew stiff from constant smiling. While satisfaction bloomed inside her.

Taking a last peek up and down the street for sign of Nila and Andy, she failed to spot them among the people filling the sidewalks. Wherever they were, they'd be fine, she told herself. She trusted Nila completely, to watch over Andy. A voice called to her as she was about to head for the barn to watch the sale. "Mrs. Pladson?"

"Yes, I'm Mrs. Pladson." She studied the young cowboy who'd caught up with her. A guitar hung from a strap over his shoulder.

"I'm a friend of Rom's, my name's Early Goodin. He said it was okay for me to come play and sing out front of the livery, draw more people to the sale? That set right with you, Mrs. Pladson?"

Her hand cupped her chin. "I've heard him mention you, I believe the two of you've played music here at the livery, a time or two? When it wasn't busy?" She tipped her head to the side, her lips pursed. "Um, yes, I suppose so. Go ahead, Son, do."

His face cracked in a wide grin. "And if a now and then person is to give me a coin for playing, is it agreeable for me to keep it?"

She considered and gave him a gentle look of warning. "Surely, yes, as long as you're polite and don't make a nuisance of yourself. Excuse me, I have to go now." Behind her as she hurried away skirts in hand, the young man had begun to strum the guitar, and in a rich, youthful voice began to sing, and play *Whoopie Ti-Yi-o, Git Along Little Dogies*. A song she'd often heard Rom picking out on his banjo. *Over and over*.

After a minute or two he burst into yodeling. She shook her head, smiling and wondering, *What next?*

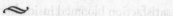

I nside the barn, benches were packed with people; quite a few watched from the rental buggies and wagons pushed to the wall, or stood. Pete, grinning, came to her with a keg turned upside down, plopped it down on the dirt floor, and motioned her to sit.

The auctioneer on the buckboard platform was a grey-haired, mustachioed older rancher, well-known in the county. After turning his ranch over to his sons, he took up auctioneering. Jocelyn was glad to have been able to hire him. His grown daughter sat at a small table next to him to record the sales. He'd been making jokes with the crowd between sales but now swung back into business as Ben Stewart came into the barn with a team of sleek grey mules, circling inside the arena slowly to show them off.

"Fine looking mule team," the auctioneer barked, "I'm at a hundred fifty, a hundred fifty, now hundred fifty, need two hundred, two hundred, now two hundred—folks, these are prime mules! Two hundred fifty, two hundred fifty, two hundred fifty... He continued without getting a higher bid. "Going, going, gone to the feller up there on the wagon seat, black hat, for two hundred fifty!"

Jocelyn's head had continually swiveled to the "Yep!" "Yep" "Yep" of the floor men in an effort to see who was bidding. Her eyes found the winning buyer waving his ticket from his seat on a wagon. She couldn't have been happier for Ben Stewart, as he led his beautiful mules from the arena. His son, Lafe, riding a large sorrel draft mule followed. One of Ruthie Freeman's helpers entered the arena next, leading a black draft mule, and the auctioneer's lively, rhythmic chant began again.

A body could almost dance to it.

At noon, the sale over, she went outside to help serve food, give at least some of her women friends a break. Mabel Goody shook her head, pushed a hot sausage in a bun into Jocelyn's hand, told Tarsy to pour her some lemonade, wrapped a cherry-hand pie in brown paper and handed it to her. "You go on out to the hotel and hear the speeches, we're doin' fine here. You've done a lot more than we have, fixin' for today. G'wan." She waved her to leave.

"I suppose I should look for my little son, and Nila. I haven't seen them since early morning."

Mabel nodded. "They're comin' right behind you."

Andy ran up to her, catching her skirts at the knees. Nila followed close behind him.

"Where have you been?" Jocelyn knelt to wrap him tight in her arms. She looked up at Nila for the answer.

Nila bit her lip, looked guilty, nervous. She took a deep breath. "We were at Mr. Cochran's fair, his picnic, behind the hotel. I hope that you don't mind. We heard children playing and went to look for just a minute. They were playing games, gunny sack races, flying Jenny on a seesaw, blowing bubbles from pans of soapy water, beanshooter and jumping rope contests for everybody, not just children. Andy—" she hesitated, "won a prize."

Jocelyn looked at him. "A prize?"

"I's cream!" he shouted. "All the 'nana I's cream I could eat." He rubbed his stomach, and laughed proudly.

"If he ate too much, Jocelyn, I'm sorry." Nila looked worried. "We also had doughnuts, apples, and fried chicken drumsticks." She wrinkled her nose. "And then there was—we had—chocolate pie, just a small slice."

Disappointment washed over Jocelyn. She wished she had a place to sit down. "J.L. provided ice cream?" She swallowed. "How? Tell me."

"Hand-cranked freezers, ten of them, worked by people in line to help. I'm not sure where he got the ice, but he had it, and the rock salt, too."

Jocelyn stood with her hand on her mouth, shaking her head. Nila looked miserable. Like there was even more on her mind, whatever it could be was making her pale. Andy spotted his father and Rom and ran to them, shouting, "I's cream!"

"There's things a lot worse than Andy and I having ice cream," Nila burst out. "Mr. Cochran heard that you were over here having the mule and horse sale only for income, not really selling out the business, at all. He's 'hound kickin' mad', as my pa used to say. Now, he's lined up a rider with a mule to race Rom on Shay this evening, and he intends to win. He was making bets against Rom with every man he could talk into it, maybe a hundred bets. Then, steaming all over the place, people heard his threats, what he intended to do to you, that people heard but wouldn't repeat to me."

"Momma, I had the bestest time." Andy had come back to catch her hand. "I'm sorry you didn't get to have I's cream, too. Everybody ate it all up."

"It's all right. I'm glad you got to have ice cream, I'm glad you had a good time. Thank you, Nila, for taking care of him for me." She ruffled his hair and pulled him close. "As long as he's here in one piece, I'm satisfied."

"Well, I brought Andy back here now because I didn't want him hurt. I didn't see a sign of it where we were, but folks are saying," she took a long deep breath, "that there's a mad dog, frothing awful at the mouth, racing wild around town today. That he's already bitten another dog that will now be sick with rabies, too." She scratched nervously at the back on her hand, then waved it in the air. "Nobody's been able to catch the dog doing this."

"What? I haven't heard about it. Or seen any such thing." Jocelyn chilled all over.

Nila bit her lip, a frown furrowed her brow. "A lot of folks are really scared, Jocelyn. At first some thought it was a wild, sick coyote, and later that it had run off and left. A man said 'no, it's a town dog'. Said that he recognized the bone-thin, greyish brown dog as belonging to a neighbor. Folks were running about, grabbing their children and leaving the picnic. Mr. Cochran was doing everything to get them to stay, begging even. Tried to make us, me and Andy, stay. He says that it isn't true, about any mad dog putting folks in danger. That there isn't anything like that and that you've spread this 'tale' to spoil the day, ruin his picnic. You didn't, did you?".

Jocelyn stared wide-eyed at her, and gave a wry laugh. "No. In the name of Sweet Hannah, I would never do that! Spread such a horrible lie to frighten everybody?" *It'd be tempting, though, if it would remove J.L. from my life.* She grabbed Andy up into her arms and motioned with her head for Nila to follow her. "We need to tell Pete, and Rom, talk to them, let everyone know. If this is true—it is serious, deadly serious."

ELEVEN

"I remember one time, when I lived back in Missouri," Nila told Jocelyn in a thin voice, "there was a mad dog running amuck." Jocelyn nodded, her heart thumping as they hurried toward the sale barn. She held Andy tighter in her arms, her cheek buried in his wispy hair.

"What happened, did the dog bite anyone?" She looked at Nila.

"Nobody got bitten that I know of, but the dog did tear into three of our neighbor's cows, biting them. The first day, the cows went kind of crazy, then their hindquarters dragged, paralyzed. Not sure how much after that the cows died. It was figured by some that a rabid possum had bit the dog in the first place, making the poor thing how it was, terrible sick."

Jocelyn panted as the three of them rushed on toward the barn, "That is so sad. I've heard of rabid coyotes biting dogs, bats can carry the disease, too." She stumbled at the sudden shrieking whinny of a horse from the pasture beyond the holding pens. Nearly dropped Andy when a gunshot sounded seconds later from the same direction. "What—in the name of Hannah?" She stopped, waited, and looked frantically toward the pasture.

"Jocelyn!" she heard Pete call and was relieved to see him striding her way. His jaw was set, his face sweaty as he took Andy, pulled her into the barn and motioned Nila to follow. "What happened out there? The gunshot?" she motioned with her head.

"I'm sorry, sweetheart." He opened his mouth, closed it, then continued, "You look like you've probably heard that a mad dog is racing every which way around town. He rampaged by here, bit your sorrel broodmare, the one you bought from Ben Stewart that he and his son delivered a while back. You called her Nell. Bit her on the leg and I think on the muzzle—left some froth there."

"The gunshot?" She had a premonition as to the answer and her stomach churned.

"That was Prank trying to shoot the cussed hound. Prank missed and the dog got away." He swallowed, his adam's apple bobbing in his throat. "Poor thing vanished before anybody could stop it. Some fellas have already taken off to find and put down the dog before it attacks another animal, or a child."

For a minute Jocelyn couldn't speak, her heart hurting. "No, not Nell! The rabid dog bit that poor mare?" Tears burned behind her eyes and she rubbed her nose. "This is my fault. I should have penned her, safe." She caught Pete's arm, her voice choking as she explained. "I staked her and the other two horse mares far out to graze in the open pasture. Because they are the ones I was keeping, I wanted the mare, Nell, and the other two, separate from the sale animals in the pens. Breed stock for more baby mules. Poor Nell." Frantic, she asked, "What can we do for her, Pete, is there anything, so that she'll live, be her sweet self again?"

He looked down at her, pain in his eyes. "There's not a lot that can be done for an animal with rabies, hon. Even if that vaccine for humans that the French doctor, Pasteur, came up with a few years ago would be available for animals, I'm afraid we'd not locate any in time to save Nell. I'm sorry as hell, Jocey."

"I want to see her." Pete caught her as she started for the back doors of the barn.

"No, honey. Us men will see to Nell. I want you to take Andy and Nila and go home to the ranch. Rom will stay here and help Prank. I'll be there soon as I can, I'll take one of the livery horses. It may take a spell to settle up with the auctioneer, help the last of the buyers to get the stock they bought onto the road. Later, if that poor mad dog hasn't been found and put out of its misery, I may help in the search."

She started to protest, that it was her business, her responsibility to stay and see to matters, her poor animal. Feeling numb in every limb, she looked down on Andy, his hand warm in hers. He was also her responsibility, the more important one. And Nila. "Fine," she said quietly, her throat dry, "we'll go."

He kissed her forehead, patted Andy, and gave Nila a solemn grin. "Y'all will be safer at home. If you see the mad dog anywhere after leaving here, you just keep right on goin', hear? I better get on back to the mare."

A short while later, Prank had hitched her mule team to her wagon and halted it close to the livery's open front doors. Jocelyn brushed straw off Andy's clothes, lifted him in, and climbed up after him. Nila followed. Prank, handed the lines to Jocelyn, and said sympathetically, "You take care goin' home, now, Missus. We'll see to your poor bitten mare, don't you worry." He waved her away. "We kin take care a' gettin' things back in order, too."

She gave him a weak smile of thanks, shook the reins over the mules, then pulled them to a halt, remembering to ask, "Where's Rom?" She had to see him before she left, probably should take him with her.

Prank scratched his whiskery jaw, his expression faint with guilt. "I let him go with them that's chasin' the foamin' dog. The young fella wasn't goin' to have it no other way, him an' the boy who played the guitar."

"The scamps, I should've known." Bouncing a curled knuckle against her mouth, she groaned. *Too late now to change the situation, have to let it go, he'd better not tangle with the crazed animal.* With a deep sigh, she tapped the reins over the mules, urging them forth, then hesitated. From the commotion coming from outside on the street, people shouting, horses neighing, Jocelyn wasn't surprised to see clattering rigs pulling free of hitch rails every which way up and down the street, drivers looking grim. Heading from town, families anxious to be home, safe. She couldn't blame them. Cochran was likely sour, the day ending early. She sat back. "Looks like we'll have to wait a few minutes for the tangle of traffic to clear so we can leave." She looked at Nila, who had a book in her lap.

"I'd intended to read this on the way home." Nila held the book up with a wry smile. "But it's no more a happy subject than rabies is. Guess I'll save it for another time."

Jocelyn read the cover, "*The Jungle* by Upton Sinclair. You came by it somehow, today?"

"Yes, Elise loaned it to me. She didn't like the book much, but thought I might and I know that I will. The book was her uncle's, he left it behind when he moved away. It's about the horrible conditions of the Chicago stockyards for both workers and the animals—the meat. Elise says it's too gory so she didn't finish it, but she heard plenty when her Pa and uncle talked about it."

"And you want to read it? You're right, it doesn't sound any more pleasurable than our awful rabies trouble."

"It's an important, popular new novel, Jocelyn. The author, Mr. Sinclair, isn't a journalist like I want to be, but he spent weeks undercover inside meat packing plants in Chicago, learning all that was going on. Readers were right away plumb nettled by what they learned from the book, mostly about the nasty way food was handled, rats, dung, and all. He'd wanted them to pay attention to dangers from the business for workers and poor treatment of the animals. He said, 'I aimed at the public's heart, and by accident hit it in the stomach.'" She beamed. "Already, because of this book and how folks feel about it, President Theodore Roosevelt insists that congress pass the U.S. Pure Food and Drug Act. American slaughterhouses are being improved right now and will be into the future."

"That's wonderful, but it really interests you, Nila?"

She nodded slowly. "It does. I like it when a book, a novel like this, can change lives, our country, for the better."

"All right then. If I ever have the time, I might want to read the book myself."

They were edging from the livery out into the street when a commotion of yelling—a shrill female voice and bark of a male—exploded next door, causing Jocelyn's mule team to toss their heads and attempt to run. "Whoa mules, steady there." She allowed them to prance a bit, holding the lines tight in her fists, then pulling them up toward her. "That's it, Alice, Zenith, good mules, you're fine." She blew a satisfied breath and looked to see what in the name of Hannah was going on at the hat shop now.

Out front of the store, Maretta ferociously cranked her motorcar again and again until it finally began to cough and rumble.

J.L., who'd been standing aside, went to climb into the motorcar on the passenger side. Maretta rushed to give him a hard shove that practically landed him on the plank walk. Hands on her hips, she gave J.L. a piercing glare. He backed up, mouth dropped open in shock.

"Oh, my." Jocelyn bit back a chuckle. *Those two at one another again.* She shook the reins, preparing to drive the team wide around the kerfuffle taking place.

"You lied," Maretta screeched, loud enough to be heard a long way up and down main street as she climbed into the motorcar. "You said that there wasn't a mad dog on the loose at all, that it was an awful lie that the Pladson woman spread in order to ruin your picnic." She blasted her horn. "I'm getting out of here."

Nila was holding her hand to her mouth, while Jocelyn, from the corner of her eye, maintained a distance from the scarlet menace, Model A Ford motorcar, safety of her mules and her loved ones high in her mind.

"Dadgummit, I thought she did tell that whopper," J.L. thundered, "one more silly-woman move to stop my plans. I didn't know there really is a mad dog around, running loose." He removed his hat and leaned on the rumbling motorcar. "Maretta, dear, I want my money, that's all. I bet a fortune on the mule race that's supposed to be happening about now. Instead, everybody's either gone off home or are out running down the damned dog. You could show a little friendly sympathy, you know." At that moment he saw Jocelyn in the wagon approaching alongside. He clapped his hat on his head and went grandly down the street.

Jocelyn laughed out loud.

The Model A lunged forward. Maretta, with one hand at the steering wheel and the other hand hanging onto her enormous flowery hat, chugged and lurched off down the street.

Still smiling, Jocelyn shook the reins, "C'mon, Alice, Zenith, let's all go home and have a nice quiet evening."

~

They had left the outskirts of Skiddy two or three miles behind when Nila gasped sharply, putting her book aside. "Jocelyn, look there. Isn't that Maretta's red Model A out in that pasture, tipped over?" She leaned forward for a better look.

"Oh my goodness, it surely looks that way." Jocelyn snapped the reins over the team's back, urging them on faster, and took in the scene ahead. For some reason, it appeared that Maretta had left the road, her motorcar taking out a quarter mile of fence. The red hulk, on its side, was being inspected by a half dozen or so curious cows. Maretta, dirty, sobbing, hat and clothes askew, wobbled up from the pasture to the road.

Chewing the inside of her cheek, Jocelyn drew her team to a stop by the miserable-looking woman. "Maretta, how are you? What on earth happened?"

Maretta gave Jocelyn an angry, studied look for a moment, swiped at her eyes. "I saw the cursed mad dog, tried to hit the despicable thing, run over it. You can blessed well see what happened." She waved her arm. "And the dog is still running loose."

"Are you hurt, though? Let me drive you back to town. Or wherever you were headed."

"I can walk, I don't need your help." She hurtled past them headed in the direction they were taking.

"What if the mad dog is close around here?" Nila leaned out from the wagon to say to her.

Jocelyn took a moment, watching the figure wobble along the road. She cleared her throat, shook the lines to get the mules moving. "It's not safe, Miss Rudd, Nila is right, the dog could be close by, still."

Maretta halted. As the team and wagon drew toward her, she started across to them, then stopped. She spoke sharply, arms waving, the expression on her face erratic. "I was on my way to my friend, Gerda Bender's. Wanted some peace from that awful hulla-baloo back in town. That pasture there, where the blessed cattle will probably be tromping all over my motorcar is Benders's property. Their home place is ahead a couple miles. I can walk there if you'll just stop bothering me."

And it's their cows you could've hit, and yes, your motorcar the red heap left in the Benders's pasture. "We can give you a lift. It'll be safer. Please." Jocelyn managed a decent tone and a hand signal for Maretta to come and get into the wagon. Nila climbed over the seat and into the back. Jocelyn pulled Andy closer to her side. They waited. A dust-devil chased along the road from a sudden breeze that also flurried Maretta's skirts.

She stood there like a statue for a minute or two, tossed her head and looked around. Likely thinking of the sick, runaway dog. Her shoulders slumped and with a deep frown she came to their wagon, climbed up on the seat next to Andy, and stared ahead.

"Are you sure you don't want to go back to town, Maretta? The Benders may not be home. At your hotel room you could get yourself together, make arrangements for retrieving your motorcar and..."

"Fine," Maretta shrieked, "take me back to town."

Jocelyn chewed the inside of her cheek, nodded, and turned her team back toward Skiddy.

"You and Maretta Rudd are friends now, I take it?" Pete said the next morning at breakfast. He'd been later than expected the night before. The marshal had already dispensed with the rabies sick dog, which had become practically dead even before it was put to an end. Pete had helped friends and their mules to right Maretta's Model A and get it back on the road. It'd been banged up, he'd said, but still driveable.

Friends? Jocelyn took her time answering. "I doubt that Maretta is ready for any such thing. I can't imagine me being friends with a person so strong-minded to put me out of business." She sighed and shook her head. "No, not friends. Just bare toleration."

A few evenings later, Rom finished eating and sat with his elbows on the supper table, wearing a wide grin and a faraway look in his eyes. Jocelyn knew he had something on his mind, and asked, "Care to share what you're thinking, Rom?'

"Are you thinking about a girl? My friend, Elise, maybe?" Nita teased, carefully watching his face.

"Not a girl," he answered blithely, then joked, "not this time." He laughed. "I'm thinkin' about Ol' Cockroach and how mad he was about 'his picnic' endin' the way it did before the day was even over, the race he planned on not happenin'. He'd bet a mighty amount on Homer Justen and his tall white mule named Boone. Bet that they'd beat me ridin' Shay. Boone is more horse than mule and can run like lightnin', which is why J.L. figgered he'd get a win for sure, an' counted heavy on makin' a pile of money. Then that poor dog come rampagin' through the whole affair, scarin' people half to death, sendin' them scatterin' hell to breakfast."

"Scattering them in the direction of their homes," Jocelyn corrected.

"Yeh, you're right, Ma." He grinned blithely at her. "I sure felt sorry for that dog, but I don't feel one shred of pity for J.L. Cockroach and his bellyachin' about the race bein' canceled. He'd probably have lost, anyhow. Shay an' me coulda' won."

"You can't be sure of that, Son." Pete reminded. "That mule, Boone, is plenty fast in a run. Might as well have wings."

"Doesn't matter, we got us another race set to run."

"Another race?" Jocelyn frowned. "I suppose this is J.L.'s idea? That man is as wily as a fox coming on a hen coop. I don't think you should have anything to do with him."

Rom wiped his mouth on the back of his hand. "I'm tired of how that bigshot treats you, Ma, so I went and challenged him to the race. I mean to poke a hole in his constant braggin' and cheatin' folks. Make a fool of him once and for all."

"That is a tall order." Pete cocked an eyebrow. "When is this race supposed to be?"

"Day after tomorrow. J.L. wanted the race to be the same as was planned for the 4th of July, Homer Justen and Boone against me and Shay. Homer had other things to do and wasn't hardly interested this time, anyway. I don't think he likes Mr. Cochran much."

A good judge of character, Jocelyn thought with a wry smile, remembering Rom's friend, Homer Justen, a tall, homely but a polite, good-hearted young man.

"If you're not racin' against the Justen boy and his mule, then who?" Pete shoved back from the table, arms across his chest, a wary expression in his eyes.

"I'm racin' against Ol' Cockroach. I bet him that I can beat him in a race, me on Shay against him in his fancy Oldsmobile."

"You what?" Jocelyn was half out of her chair. "You and Shay can't outrun a motorcar. Those awful noisy machines travel twelve to fourteen miles an hour, some up to twenty miles an hour. Shay'd wear out in four or five miles, the Oldsmobile would be putting along still, ahead."

Pete pulled her back down. "This is a fool's bet you've made, Rom."

"And you have little if any money to put up considering what we pay you for helping out at the livery." Jocelyn rubbed her forehead. "I can't imagine J.L. betting with you direct. What are the stakes, anyhow? What if you don't win?"

"I didn't bet no money. The bet is that if I win, the windbag has to kiss my mule, Shay."

"Poor Shay," Nila said quietly, looking down at her plate.

"If I lose, I kiss Cochran's boots. That's all." Rom hitched his shoulder and was silent for a moment, the confidence in his eyes lessening only a little. "Shay will do anything I ask him to do, that mule can run like h— the dickens, I know he can. It's a rough ride, when he gallops, but I want to run that race. I gotta try, I believe sure as I'm sittin' here that I could win—Shay could win."

"There may be the simple bet between you and Cochran, but for darn sure he'll be collecting bets in town from others, that he can beat you and Shay, motorcar against mule. Where is this race to be run?" Pete stroked his jaw, concern in his eyes.

"From the edge of town out toward that farm J.L. bought, the Ivers place, the poor folks that he cheated, and had to leave with next to nothin'."

"That's about five miles, you don't intend to race that far, I hope? That'd be really hard on a galloping mule."

"The race will end at the first curve in the road, that'd be about three-quarters of a mile, maybe. I'm not gonna ruin Shay." His expression turned smart-alecky, "just ruin the cockroach, if I can."

Jocelyn looked at Pete and he looked at her,

eyebrows raised. She knew blessed well that he could read her mind. That if there was a chance J.L. Cochran would lose, be made to look the fool, if in some unusual way it would discourage him right out of town, if not the whole of Kansas, she was all for it. But, a race between a mule and his fancy motorcar?

Moments later, Rom had headed outside to start evening chores. Pete, about to follow, hesitated and said to Jocelyn, "It's a good lesson for the boy, that sometimes you lose and you take it like a man. But I'd rather do anything than kiss J.L.'s boots. I pure couldn't."

"Rom has gone through enough rough times in his young life, I think he's already learned a'plenty about losing. What I'd like to see, but I don't expect to happen, is for that greedy, gambling idiot, J.L. to kiss that Shay-mule. You know where." She said, earnestly, "Don't you?"

"Yes, you bet your life I do." He touched her cheek. "Right now, sweetheart, I got work to do."

She followed him to the porch, and saw grey rain clouds hovering in the huge stretch of sky beyond the barn. *A light shower will do my new garden good if it comes this way, but I surely don't want no more flooding like we had a month or so ago. Although the fool race tomorrow would be canceled if it did. I'd be thankful for that.*

TWELVE

E ven though yesterday's downpour of rain was a thing of the past, Jocelyn still wasn't sure that the race between Rom's mule and J.L. Cochran's shiny black and orange Oldsmobile was a good idea. No matter how the race turned out, though, it was a pretty day for it now. From horizon to horizon the sky was a brilliant blue, the Flint Hills an undulating sea of tallgrass, the sun blazing overhead.

She wasn't surprised to see that a right smart number of folks were walking from town to watch the race from the wayside. For the moment she enjoyed nodding and waving to watchers as she and Pete drove in their wagon for the curve in the road that would be the finish line of the race—choosing to watch from there. "It's a nice day today, but from the looks of this muddy road from yesterday's rain, I would have thought J.L. would've called the race off," she said as the wagon bumbled from rut to rut behind their dauntless mule team. She pulled her skirts close as the wagon splashed through muddy pools and water flew.

"Rom thought so, too, but old J.L. wasn't about to call the competition off 'because of a little mud'. He knows darned well what he's getting into but is too stubborn to see the truth of it. You have to consider, too, that if he wins, the damn fool will make a near fortune off the bets he'll collect." Pete loosened his collar, wiped his sweaty forehead with an arm, a tightness in his expression. "Too blamed many have bets on him and the fancy motorcar, against Rom and his mule."

"I half wish I'd stayed back in town with the crowd waiting to see the race start," Jocelyn lamented, "but I reckon I want to see how it ends more. Can't be in two places at once." She waved at a pair of young boys waiting for the race by the side of the road, and moments later a young couple and their three children. Of all the people she'd seen, in the crowd back in town and along the road, Maretta Rudd wasn't among them. Some said that she had an important hat order to fill—and that was reasonable.

Little Andy was spending the day with Mabel Goody, and Nila had to work at the hotel, much as she wanted to be here.

Once they'd found their spot and Pete drew the mules to a halt, minutes ticked by. The silence occasionally broken by the soft murmurs of folks waiting, a purple martin's pleasant singing and the chittering of sparrows as they flitted about in the roadside brush and flint rocks. Jocelynn was about to give up watching back along the way for sight of Rom on the mule and J.L. in his motorcar. *Maybe something happened at the starting point to derail the race, stop it cold?* A while later, from the corner of her eye, she thought she saw movement far down the muddy road.

She looked again, watched the movement take identifiable shape.

"I think I see them." Her heart pounded as she grabbed Pete's arm, pointing out the Oldsmobile that to her resembled a giant black-widow spider with orange dot on the belly. The slim figure on a mule that seemed to be painted in the muddy road, neither hardly moving.

"Yep, that's them."

"They're coming so slow."

"Dealin' with the mud. Look now, J.L. has pulled ahead."

"He has, but that's because he took the whole middle of the road. He practically forced Rom into the ditch, Pete!"

"I see it." He caught her hand in a squeeze.

A few minutes of silence followed as both Jocelyn and Pete strained to see.

"Whoa," she cried, "J.L., swerved his motorcar and nearly hit Rom and Shay. Oh, good, now the Oldsmobile looks stuck." Moments later she clasped her palms tightly together, bouncing on the wagon seat like a child. "Rom and Shay have come around him. C'mon, Son, c'mon, mule." She clapped her hands and laughed. "You can do this!" She waited, hardly breathing. "Just sit there in the mud, Mr. Cochran, you have it coming."

A moment later, Pete pounded his thigh with his fist. "Damn it to hell, J.L. has got the Oldsmobile goin' again, he's movin'. Lordy, look at him come," he pointed, "mud or no mud. Catchin' up to Rom." The atmosphere was charged with feeling. "Passed Rom, now," Pete muttered, "takin' the whole road again. Don't see the boy. He has to be back there, somewhere."

Jocelyn's hand went to her chest, her eyes straining to see more than the large open motorcar plunging through the mud toward them, a giant insect, coming closer. "Rom," she whispered, "please be fine." She glared at the black Oldsmobile, wishing this wasn't happening.

"I'll be a son-of-a-gun." Pete laughed. "Look at that!" Just a short distance before the finish line, Cochran's Oldsmobile had rolled into a deep hole, thick, clayey mud up to the fenders, the motorcar rattling and shaking but clearly stuck again. J.L. revved the engine a couple more times before it coughed and quit.

"Twelve yards yet from the bend in the road, and there comes Rom," Jocelyn said with a teary laugh. Her heart thundered and she began to squeal and yell like she hadn't since she was a child. "Oh, Pete, I think he's going to make it." Arms around one another's waist, they watched their boy on his mule trot easily through the mud, and around the bend, and back again to the sound of loud cheering from those close at hand. Cochran climbed from his motorcar into knee deep mud, cursing equally loud.

"Pa," Rom called, "you got a rope there in the wagon so me an' Shay can pull this gent's motorcar outta the mud?" He climbed down, gave his mule a long hug, and patted him, talking softly.

"I can unhitch," Pete replied, "rig the team to his motorcar and get it outta there." He climbed down from the wagon beaming, and Jocelyn followed, her hands clasped together in pure joy.

"Nah, no need to unhitch, Pa. Me and Shay can

take care of it. If the Oldsmobile was in the ditch, I'd say use the team, but I can get it outta the mudhole."

Smart boy, Jocelyn was thinking. His mule saw her coming and *eee-onked* a loud greeting. She hugged Shay's neck, stroked his muzzle. "You did good, really good, Shay." She lowered her voice, "Beating that rascal and his motorcar." Shay twisted his head to nuzzle her shoulder, lips drawn back in a mule smile. She laughed. "Yes, I'll have carrots for you when we get home, sugar cubes, too. You remember being my frisky little pet once, don't you?" Jocelyn gave him a last stroking and stepped back out of the way.

Close by, J.L. yanked a cigar from a vest pocket. He shook with anger and the cigar slipped from his fingers and fell into the mud. A deeper fury rushed into his face, turning it red. "You've got a smart mouth, sonny boy!" He stomped through the muck, glowering at Rom who was taking the rope from Pete in preparation to hitch the motorcar to the mule's harness.

"An' you owe my mule a big smackeroo, 'cause we won," Rom taunted him with a grin. "I got to the finish line, already."

J.L. gave Rom a flinty look of hate, for a few seconds too angry to find his voice. "It wasn't a completed race, so you didn't win, and even if you had've I wouldn't kiss anybody's mule. Ever."

"An' my mule will be happy about that. Despite the deal you made." He added, suppressing a laugh, "I came around your motorcar slicker than cow slobbers an' won fair and square. Sorry, Mr. Cochran, but I didn't put your motorcar in this mudhole, you did."

"Get a horse," George Jacobsen yelled from the sidelines, laughing. Back in town, Jocelyn remembered,

George had locked the doors on the feed store for the short duration of the race. The chant was picked up and repeated over and over, "get a horse", "get a horse..."

Others who'd watched from the finish line ignored J.L.'s anger and came to congratulate Rom. One fellow slapped him on the back and said, "I didn't bet either way, but if I had, it would've been placed on you and that mule, there. Mules is smart and better transportation than one of them motor-thingamajigs, any day."

Another man walked up and said to Pete, heading through mud to give Rom a hand, "I saw what the gent did wrong." He was looking toward Cochran who was fuming as he swiped at mud clinging to his trouser legs and accomplished little. "I watched him pick his way on the road, he drove right into the trail showing the most travel ruts, thinkin' it'd be the best. That's wrong. Mud's just been cut deeper and more where it's been used so much and you're damn sure goin' to get stuck drivin' one of them new motor contraptions in it."

A tall thin man picking his teeth with a whittled matchstick added, "An' a mule will go around or plumb through it, with no never mind."

"No question about that." Pete clapped him on the shoulder, nodded to the other men, and went to help Rom finish up with the hitching. That done, he continued on to join those grouped behind the Oldsmobile to push.

As they worked, Cochran paced, waving his arms, patting his chest pocket where there were no more cigars. He looked mad enough to kill somebody. Yelled for the umpteenth time at those throwing their strength behind his motorcar to free it from the mud, "That motorcar is worth a damn fortune. Be careful, dammit!"

Jocelyn pressed her fist against her mouth. Praying that if he couldn't just disappear into nowhere that he'd at least shut up, or as Rom would say "hitch his lip". Every man in the lot of them had better sense than J.L. Cochran.

Rom slapped Shay's side and urged, "C'mon, mule, get up there—that's it, pull hard, mule. You got the stuff, c'mon." Men grunted as they pushed in back, again, and again. The motor car budged a foot or so. After several more attempts, the motorcar had begun to leave the mud, then slid back, further.

Cochran rushed forward, carrying a thick muddy stick to where Shay, with all his mule power was straining to pull, and whacked the mule on the back, hard, making Shay jerk and try to run. "Pull, pull you lazy, good for nothing mule." He lifted the stick a second time and Rom leaped and caught J.L.'s arm, twisting it until Cochran howled and dropped the stick.

"Leave the cussed motorcar where it is, that's what I'd do," a man watching called out. "That fool don't deserve no help."

Jocelyn muttered, "If that isn't the truth, I've never heard it."

"Don't you hit my mule," Rom gritted, ducking Cochran's fist like a pro. "He's doing the best he can. If you leave him be, he'll haul your consarned contraption free. Now move out of our way."

"You don't tell me what to do, you half-grown imbecile." Cochran gave Rom's shoulder a hard shove.

Jocelyn, her mouth dropped, took a step forward, itching to intervene and pound Cochran to pieces herself. Tension in the air was taut as a fiddle string about to break. Her heartbeat quickened, watching.

At the back of the motor car, Pete wore a tight grin. "It's your mule, Son, an' your say." His blazing eyes declared that he'd jump into the fray if he had to. As did George Jacobsen standing next to him, his flinty expression also aimed at Cochran.

Foolishly ignoring them, Cochran stooped and snatched up the stick and aimed for Shay again.

"I said, don't hit my mule!" Rom charged at him with his fists drawn but Pete got to J.L. first, swung his fist back and slammed it into J.L.'s face. Blood spurted from his nose, his sharp grunt and babbled curses at Pete were negated by his hands clasped to his face as he stumbled, moaning, in a circle.

"You don't ever hit an animal, especially one that's working its hardest for you. Nor do you shove my boy around when he's helping you." Pete jabbed a hand through his hair, his jaw rigid. "For lord's sake, everybody settle down and we'll get this man's fancy nuisance out of the mud and head the damn thing in the right direction."

Cochran, wiping blood on his shirt sleeve, continued his mumbling complaints. "I'll sue for assault, you ignorant yokels will pay for any damage you do to my Oldsmobile."

Pete left off pushing the motorcar and grabbed J.L. by the shirt front, "You don't blame your confounded motorcar troubles on my son, or his mule." He was about to punch Cochran again when, at Jocelyn's frown and shake of her head, he dropped his fist to his side and returned to the task at hand, next to George, of removing the motor car. The gang's pushing plus two more of Shay's herculean pulls and the Oldsmobile came free with a loud sucking sound onto firmer ground. A deep sigh of relief traveled through everyone watching. Those who'd worked getting the motorcar free grinned, clapped one another on the shoulder, and stomped mud from their boots.

J.L., his bloody face scowling, still ramped at Rom. "Damn you, boy, you're the one wanted this race, asked for it. Look what you done to my vehicle. You didn't win fair, truth is, you didn't win at all but I'm going to be held to losing. Have to dig up every dime I've got to pay off the bets—when I sure as hell shouldn't have to— your fault, all of it." He lunged at Rom and Shay's hoof flashed in a sideways kick that caught Cochran in the left thigh. He fell to the ground, rolling and screaming. "My leg's broken. Shoot the damn mule." He pointed. Nobody moved. "Somebody got a gun?" He croaked, almost a sob, "Mule could've killed me." He crawled about in the mud, trying to get up, and sat back. Color except for the blood, had left his face. Moaning, his mouth in a grimace, he rubbed his leg.

"At least the mule finished his work gettin' the horseless carriage outta the mud before givin' the gripin' loudmouth his due," a raised voice announced.

"Thinkin' that myself." George's smile bloomed and he shook the man's hand.

Pete knelt over Cochran and checked his left thigh, feeling the limb carefully while Cochran howled. "Sorry you got kicked, J.L. but that's another thing about mules, they're smart and they know when they are wronged. Or that the person who treats them kindly has been wronged. They kick. Wonder it didn't happen already." His brows pulled in. "You're going to have a long stretch of pain in that thigh, likely, and have a hell of a bad bruise and trouble getting around for a while, but your leg ain't broke that I can tell. So shut up, for god's sake, and let me help you stand up." Rom jumped to help on J.L.'s other side.

J.L.'s jaw sagged with complaint as he hopped on one foot, his hand to his thigh, "I can't drive my Oldsmobile with my leg paining like this. How the hell will I get home, get my Olds home? Start it even?" He moaned, practically fell into Pete. With Rom's help, they got J.L. into his Oldsmobile onto the orange seat on the passenger side.

Pete looked around for somebody to offer to drive. Nobody did, likely because they didn't know how. "I've never driven one of these things, either, but if you'll tell me what to do—and I already know how to crank it to get the motorcar started, I'll get you back to Skiddy and to home." He turned to Jocelyn, "You follow driving the wagon, and when we get Mr. Cochran settled in, and have Doc Asherwood have a look at him to be sure his leg ain't broke, we can pick up Nila and head on back to the ranch, and for Andy at Mabel's."

"Sure." Jocelyn went to the wagon, climbed up and waited, while Pete cranked the motorcar, again and again until the engine finally chugged to life. He climbed in beside J.L. who was shakily lighting up a cigar, found likely in a coat pocket. They talked for several minutes, then Pete was turning the black sketchy vehicle with its orange seat—how much it reminded her of a black widow spider—slowly in the road, back toward Skiddy. She heaved a sigh of relief, released the brake, clicked her tongue, and Alice and Zenith were off, following down the muddy, messy road.

THIRTEEN

J ocelyn asked that night as they prepared for bed, "What was it like, Pete, driving J.L.'s motorcar— his Oldsmobile and him, back to Skiddy?" She turned the blanket back on their bed, and started on the tiny buttons of her shirtwaist.

He heaved a sigh and rubbed his jaw in thought. "It was kinda' exciting, to be truthful, traveling the road that fast. It was almost as comfortable as seated on a saddled horse. But not quite," he added, seeing her frown. "Getting stuck in the mud how it did is a darn-sure problem with motorcars."

"And it was a mule, it was Shay, and Rom directing him that saved the day and pulled it out," she reminded quickly, chin lifted in pride.

"The biggest problem of all with a motorcar is that hardly anybody has the money to buy something like that, fun as it might be to have." He unbuttoned his shirt and pulled it off.

"If they did," she said, "they'd be smart enough to

put it back into their farm or ranch—buy more land, more stock animals, use it to hire on help, I'm sure. A good life can be made that way. Hasn't it already, for centuries?" She stepped out of her shoes and unfastened her skirt. "The same amount of money for a motorcar could likely put a body into a business that'd support them for life."

"You're right, there, honey." He gave her a peck on the cheek, but she wasn't finished with what she needed to know about J.L., yet.

"I wonder, when he's on his feet again, if J.L. might finally move on, not stay around in Skiddy? Give up on muddy country roads and stubborn but right-thinking small-town folk?" She held her breath, her spirits lifting in hope.

"I wouldn't count on that, sweetheart. He didn't talk like he's figuring to do any such thing. Nope. Cochran griped to the skies that his injured leg might slow him down in his plans to have a house built—on one of those properties he practically stole from poor folks." Pete pulled off his boots and shook his head. "Hate to tell you this, hon, but he also boasted that he's intending to run for the council seat that Mrs. Noack is leaving. Darn fool had the gall," he pulled off a sock, "or maybe ignorance," he pulled off the other sock and tossed it aside, "to ask for my vote. I laughed at him, couldn't help it."

"Good grief, no, Pete! Running for office on the town council, and building a house?" She popped up through the neckline of her nightgown and straightened the rest of it in place. "That means he's staying on. Unless—he's building the house to sell? I worry less about any chance he has at a city council seat. Nobody but a fool would vote for him." *If luck held out*.

Pete took off his pants and stood there in his long johns. "I doubt that the house is to sell. He's as crooked as a dog's hind leg, though, so maybe the law will have something to do with his future, like behind bars."

"That would be a good thing, before he causes any more trouble, cheating folks, trying to ruin me and the livery." Jocelyn crawled into bed, deciding to discuss the matter with the marshal, and or his wife, Deputy Cora, next trip to Skiddy. She'd ask Cora about Maretta, too, who was behaving oddly—rarely seen on the street these days, ducking out of sight at times, avoiding being seen for some odd reason. *Hiding from something? Somebody?*

Jocelyn had almost given up having a conversation with Maretta, and any effort to be friends. Her mind turned to Pete as he came to the bed. Smiling, she scooted over for him to slide in beside her.

❦

For three weeks, J.L. Cochran was confined to his hotel room, healing from the kick that Shay had, blessedly to Jocelyn's mind, given him. A peaceful period during which she had a second, smaller but profitable mule sale, and made two more short distance mule-buying trips. Plus catching up with work at home with Nila's help. To her disappointment, when she had a free moment to talk, Cora was out of town or Jocelyn was away when Cora was available.

"Maretta is nervous as a bug in a bucket with the pump about to flow, that's for sure," Cora agreed, when

Jocelyn finally had a chance to visit the marshal's office and discuss the matter with her. "For one thing, she's counted on J.L. to protect her from trouble and he's laid up for now." Cora leaned back in her chair behind the desk. "he's not there to help if she needs it. I suspect that something from her past is about to catch up on her, and she's afraid. That happens sometimes, with women alone." Cora pinched her lip and at Jocelyn's motion to continue, her hand dropped to her lap. "I told her she could call on me, or the marshal, if she was in real danger and needed help."

"Did she tell you what the problem might be, if it was real serious?" *Likely it had something to do with her connection to J.L., as much as they were at each other's throat. Or was it something else?*

"Actually, worried as she behaves, Maretta pretty much tosses it off as nothing. Said she'd come to Skiddy to get away from an abusive suiter who was trying to force her into marriage. That sometimes she 'gets the willies' thinking he might be around. That he's looking for her, you know. She promised to come to me or the marshal if serious trouble did come."

"I see." *Maybe that's the truth of it and maybe it isn't.* "J.L. may be up and around soon and she'll have less to worry about if she sees him as protection." *And I'll likely have more.*

Sooner than she would have liked, J.L. was back on his feet. Getting around with a cane, he was in and out of his businesses but more often on the street confabulating with folks. Still trying to worm his way onto the town council, "In the name of progress, important to the survival of this town."

Cane in hand, limping from one business to

another, spending no little time in the saloons, he preached over and over that Maretta's and his's accidents with their motorcars had nothing to do with their driving skills or with their excellent vehicles in general. The problem was clearly the roads, the terrible roads, not his Oldsmobile. Might even have something to do with Maretta's Ford ending up in the pasture, too.

"The country roads are an enormous problem", he expounded from his place in the audience at a town council meeting. "Roads could be improved, a fact that should be looked into and would be, in my hands, if I were on the council board. To welcome the new and much needed mode of travel: the fast and dependable motorcar."

To Jocelyn and Pete, also in the audience at the meeting, too many citizens in attendance nodded agreement—if not a nod of falling asleep.

"Every man needs a motorcar," he trumpeted. "Every sensible gentleman will soon own an Oldsmobile, a Buick, Packard, Cadillac, or a Model A Ford, and they and their lady will never be happier than with this new mode of transportation, I guarantee."

"Sure we will," Pete mumbled to Jocelyn, "if everybody stumbles on a gold mine of a sudden and has money to burn."

~

Why did a man of Cochran's ilk have to be somewhat right, in at least a few instances? Jocelyn wondered irritably, watching from the wide doors of the livery stable as a group of men gathered around the rancher, Sam McCreary's new motorcar, a shiny dark green Packard parked a short distance down the street. *Might as well eavesdrop,* she decided. Her arms crossed tight across her chest and biting her lip, she headed that way, stopping a few feet away.

From how J.L. was gloating, clambering closer to the group, talking over them as he admired the Packard, giving it a pat here and there, a body would think he'd given birth to it. "I knew it. I knew the big change has come. This," he patted McCreary's green charm, "is proof that Skiddy will be an example that the motorcar is now the way of the world. All you folks," with a wave of his arm and a hungry, beaming expression, he included the men around him, "will want to buy a motorcar. Must possess one. Horses and wagons, and the dumb mule, will become useless, things of the past."

Jocelyn moved a few steps closer, one hand gripping the other wrist behind her back, her jaw set, looking for a chance to break into the conversation and add her opinion to the goings-on. They'd be aghast at a woman's interference, to what she wanted to say to them in particular, but she just couldn't walk away as though she had no mind, or right, to know a thing or two and speak it.

Sam McCreary, with a disdainful expression directed at J.L., said, "Hell with that, Cochran. I bought this thing here," he motioned toward his new purchase, "for just a plaything. A present to my wife she'll get a kick out of—even at that, it's not somethin' to brag about. I'm aware of the troubles comin' with it. It breaks down, who fixes it? I don't know a blame thing about that. Run off the road somehow, or mired in mud, I'll have to go for a horse or mule to pull the damn thing back on the road."

J.L. tried to break in but McCreary wasn't finished. "I'll tell you this—I'm keepin' and usin' my horses and mules for the work no rancher or farmer can do without, an' a blockheaded city feller don't understand. There's a lot this pretty Packard couldn't in any way perform. I don't doubt that there may come a day when a machine will be invented that'll end the need for horse or mule power, plowin', plantin' an' harvestin', but it sure as hell ain't happenin' any time soon. Sorry to tumble you off your soapbox, Mr. Cochran, but that's how I damn well see it."

Most of the men in the group nodded their heads in agreement, expressions of dismissal directed at Cochran.

J.L.'s face went slack. Breaking eye contact with Sam, he looked around at the others. "Well, we don't know for sure about that, do we? Change can come on pretty damn fast," he offered hope with a weak smile. "I say, 'the day of the motorcar is here, right now.'" He smacked the Packard's fender.

I say you're wrong about motorcars for everybody, here and now. And if you think all your blarney this summer will get you on the town council come election, I have strong doubts about that, too. Jocelyn stood with foot patting, her hands on her hips, watching J.L. Cochran's audience begin to drift away. Feeling that Sam had taken care of the matter for now, she headed back to the livery barn, humming a tuneless something quietly to herself—her worries eased but not quite buried.

The livery stable's pastures were starting to be too grazed down. Jocelyn had finished another mule sale, this one intended to be an aid to the pastures' recovery. Shading her eyes against the bright sun, the other hand on her hip, she stood back, happily watching buyers, farmers and ranchers, herd the mules they'd bought from her through the gate and onto the dusty street, on their way out of town. Gradually, the sale barn and holding corrals were emptying. She knew even without a final counting that her earnings today would pay off her bank loan and the livery business would be hers free and clear.

From the corner of her eye, Jocelyn saw a tall, black-hatted man ambling from the emptying sale barn. *You're a bit late, if you're looking for a mule. Today's been a bang-up sale of the finest mules to be had.* She took a closer look at the man and gasped. *For Hannah's sake, if it wasn't Pete's rowdy friend and their some-times-hired hand, Red Miller.* Tall, gangly, easily recognized by his bushy, rust-colored moustache, he grinned widely and tipped his hat to her. Rom was right behind him, grinning like the cat that got the mouse and the cheese, both.

"Red Miller, if you don't beat all," she declared with a soft chuckle. "What're you doing at my mule sale and not showing off down in Oklahoma at the 101 Ranch Wild West Show? My mule stock is gone, if you're here for mules. You're late."

"I'm not here for a mule," he answered in his usual bellowing twang, "I'm here to see you, pretty lady. And ol' Pete an' the young'uns. Just a visit for a while, is all."

He drew her into a hug that lifted her off the ground. "Put me down you fool." She tried not to laugh and shoved at his shoulders. "Half the county has their eyeballs glued to your foolishness," she said of the last few stragglers leaving with their mules. "I'm the boss here and you're shocking folks."

Rom laughed as Red released her. "He's just glad to see you, Ma."

"I'm happy to see him, too." Her hands gripped her elbows. "But I prefer my feet earthbound. How are you, Red? Pete's going to be tickled to see you. Tonight, at supper, you have to tell us all about the fancy Oklahoma ranch you're working for—you're still with the 101 Ranch?"

He hesitated, removed his hat, scratched through his red hair. "Sort of, off and on." He left it at that, grinned and clapped his hat back on his now tousled hair.

Well, that pretty much covered everything about Red Miller, 'sort of, off and on'. Saddle bum was another way of looking at a man like Red. Still, she liked him—in some ways.

"I see. You have to excuse me, Red, take a look around at the livery for a bit if you want to. I have work to do, and need to tie up sales details before I can head home." She hesitated, hoped that he didn't mind.

"I believe I'll ride on out to the Nickel Hill, give Ol' Pete a howdy and give him a hand at whatever he's doin'." He gave her a wide, expectant grin.

"He's cutting kaffir if he finished with the alfalfa. I'm sure he'd welcome your giving him a hand putting it up. I should have left Rom home to help Pete, but I needed him here to assist with the mule sale."

"Be glad to help Ol' Pete. You comin' with me?" Red looked at Rom.

From the expression on his face, Rom would give anything to ride out with Red, but he shook his head. "I'll be there directly. Work to do here, for Ma."

Jocelyn had been about to say that Rom could go ahead to the ranch, with Red, if he wanted, that she and Prank could take care of chores at the livery. Instead, she smiled. She liked how he was growing up, accepting responsibility. She should allow him that. "Thanks, Son. I can use your help."

In the following hour and a half, Jocelyn settled up with the auctioneer and bid him goodbye until the next time, helped Prank and Rom with the cleaning of the stable, and put the hay barn, where the sale was held, back in order. She went over today's figures twice and smiled at the results.

In the back of her mind, as she and Rom headed for home in the wagon sometime later under a setting sun, she kept thinking about Red, that she was glad to see him, it had been quite a while. Pete would be as happy to see his old friend as a dog with two tails. But she also dreaded Red's heavy drinking, and his oft repeated efforts to draw Pete into joining him in his carousing Saturday nights. Pete, since they married, usually turned down Red's invitation to what they once considered a natural part of a cowboy's life. Red surely wouldn't turn to their son, Rom, get him started down a fool's trail?

No, Red knew better than that, he'd know that she'd skin him alive if he tried.

She chided herself for jumping to conclusions. Red might've grown out of all that. And besides—she looked over at Rom driving half asleep, letting the mules have their head—Rom was mostly a sensible young man who had a right to his own decisions.

FOURTEEN

"Mighty good, Jocelyn." Red Miller shoveled a second large forkful of gingerbread into his mouth, a splotch of thick cream ending up in his rusty-colored whiskers. Jocelyn nodded a thank you in his direction, and smiled to herself with pride. Her menfolk, Pete, Red, and Rom, would've preferred to sit out on the porch to share their windies. Or take them yonder up by the barn. *Blamed if she was going to let them get away with that.* Fortunately, they'd fallen for her coaxing them to pull up to the kitchen table and have themselves coffee and chunks of gingerbread dabbed with sweetened cream while she finished fixing supper.

By no means was she going to miss what Red was saying about the famous 101 Ranch if she didn't have to. *Did it turn out that he was related to the three Miller brothers who owned the ranch, and ran the big show?* She doubted it but one could never know. She stirred the gravy and moved the platters of steak more quietly to the warming oven, so that she could hear what Red was saying.

"The One—that's what some folks down on the 101 Ranch calls the place—is somethin' ya can't picture without seein' it. Around a hundred thousand acres, the place has its own railroad for the convenience of folks, freight cars and Pullmans." Red got up and poured himself more coffee, and added to Pete's. He continued in his booming twang, "There ain't another place like it, nowhere."

Jocelyn's hand with the spoon stilled, trying to picture such things—a railroad part of a ranch. It would be handy, to get from here to there on a ranch as huge as the 101, so it made some sense.

"There's schools," Red continued after a long draught of coffee, "churches, and more miles of roads on the 101 Ranch than a body can count. Besides the great show they been puttin' on since last year, they have farmers growin' thousands of acres of wheat, corn, other grain, and hay. They got orchards. Peaches, cherries, and apples." He waved his arm. "A cider mill, even. There's a tannery, a packing plant, and chicken farms on the One Hundred and One—they raise everything needed to feed over three hundred people who live and work there. Yep, three hundred." He took a deep breath, savoring their expressions of amazement.

"And cattle and horses, what about them?" Rom gulped down his last bite of gingerbread and gave Red an excited, studious look.

"I ain't sure about the numbers of cattle they raise, or the ranch hands that see to them, but it's a many. You can figure thousands of head of cattle, horses, mules, an' there's even buffalo on their range." He took another gulp of coffee and sat back. "They kill a beef every day to feed everybody that lives on the ranch. You ever heard of anything like that? Butcherin' a beef every day for the supper table?"

"For durn sure not." Rom's eyes were about to pop.

"Me, neither." Pete agreed with a sideways grin. "Never heard of anything like that in Kansas, and not here at Nickel Hill for blamed sure."

The men moved their chairs back as Nila came with a stack of plates to set the table. Little Andy helped with forks, his bright blue eyes just level with the tabletop.

"How could they do all that?" Nila wanted to know a minute or two later, bringing a platter of steaming fried steaks to the table. "Did the family have loads of inherited money, or something—a gold mine?"

Red grinned at her, crossed his legs and took the makings of a cigarette from his pocket and for the moment gave his attention to that. Studying, maybe for what he wanted to say.

"Pretty interesting answers to that question—the way I've always heard it," Pete put in. "The old man, George Miller, also known as Colonel Miller, was a smart, hardworking Kentuckian who traded some cured hog meat for a bunch of rangy longhorns. That was his start, Nila, and not much of one. He moved his ranch a few times, increasin' what he owned with each move. First in Missouri, then to Baxter Springs here in Kansas, finally to the Cherokee Outlet which is now Oklahoma. His one hundred thousand acres was leased from the Ponca tribe. Never been sure where he got his name for the ranch from, maybe that number of acres?" He stroked his jaw. "The old man, George Washington

Miller, his full name, died three years ago, I think I heard it was from pneumonia." He took a moment, then looked at Jocelyn and winked. "His smart wife, Molly, had the ranch turned into a trust for her three sons. Joe, the oldest, she put in charge of the whole operations and farming, Zack head cattleman, and George handles the 101 Ranch money affairs."

"He had to've been a great old guy," Red agreed, chin lifted blowing out a puff of cigarette smoke, "to build that ranch like he done. Providin' work and a fine place to live for so many folks. His wife is a fine lady, and smart, like Pete said. It was Missus Miller's luck that the Colonel left her insurance that she was able to use buildin' the White House, what they call the big house on the ranch, where she lives and entertains folks. Famous people come from near everywhere to see the ranch workins' and the shows. The cowboys on the ranch was always competin' against one another—who could stay on a buckin' bronc the longest, bust and tie a steer the fastest an' so on. But the big show, the real show, was last year."

"'Oklahoma's Gala Day', they called it," Pete put in. "What a show those ranch hands and Indians must have put on." He laughed. Moving out of the way as Nila put a heaping bowl of steaming potatoes 'in the skins' on the table.

"Well enough, this is all very interesting but it's time we ate our supper." Jocelyn motioned everyone to the table. "I didn't cook all this for nothing."

In a few minutes of silence other than scraping chairs, Jocelyn and Nila finished putting food on the table and everyone began to eat. Jocelyn was only mildly offended when Red broke the silence to say,

"The good folks at the 101 Ranch treat folks real well, cookin' up beefsteaks big as saddlebags." No matter that Nickel Hill's steaks weren't 'saddlebag' size. They were tasty, tender, and filling.

"I've heard a girl rider is part of the 101 Ranch Real West show, did you meet her?" Jocelyn put her fork aside to ask. "I think her name is Lucille Mulhall. Did you see her perform?" Andy had eaten the gravy off his potatoes, and pushed his plate toward her for more. She complied and whispered to him, "You need to eat your peas, too, Son. Remember when we picked them from the garden and you helped me shell them?"

The way you're looking at me, little man, I'm not asking you to eat cow pile from the barnyard. Now eat up. Peas, too.

He carefully put two peas on the tines of his fork, gulped them down making a face, and smiled at her.

She gave up and turned her attention to Red.

"You bet I met Lucille, saw that young lady practicin' there at the ranch a'plenty. The other riders told me that when the show went to New York and performed at Madison Square Garden—she was the hit of the show. Put some of them cowboys to shame riding' a buckin' bronco an' ropin' and tyin' a steer. Met Will Rogers, too, not a regular at the 101, but he drops in now and then to perform with the rest of them. Can't nobody rope as well as him. He can rope a rider and horse at the same time using two ropes. At the same time," he repeated, "with two ropes."

"Where is the 101 Ranch, exactly?" Rom asked suddenly, deep interest in his voice.

"Not far over the Kansas border, on the Salt Fork of the Arkansas River," Pete said.

"A few days ride on a horse," Red added, planting his fork in a cut of steak.

For the rest of the meal, Jocelyn worried about Rom's question. *Was he thinking of leaving them, riding off to Oklahoma to the 101 Ranch to maybe take part in their Real West Show? He was good with horses and mules, could do every side of ranch work, when a body thought about it. He'd taught his mule Shay a half dozen or more clever tricks. He might fit in right well at the 101, but he was too young. She'd miss him so much. Someday he'd want to go out on his own, build the life he'd like, but not yet.*

When the boy caught her staring at him, Jocelyn looked away quickly, then back at him. He grinned at her, his easy-going affectionate grin and she smiled back. *He wouldn't leave them, maybe he'd spend the rest of his life right here at Nickel Hill. I was a silly woman to think he might, and if he did take such a notion to leave, now, they'd sure be able to convince him to wait, a few more years at least.*

Pressing a subtle palm to her heart, she cleared her mind. She was suddenly interested that Red Miller had changed the subject from the 101 Ranch to the Currans, Daniel and Adella, his and Pete's bosses years back on the 7Cs Ranch.

"Took me a quick ride up there for a visit. They had money for me, and had sold a horse I'd left there. Remember that liver chestnut, Pete? Darn good horse but couldn't bring them all when I come here to work for you."

Jocelyn had met the Currans before she and Pete married. "How are Daniel and Adella, Red?"

"Fine, just fine."

"The young man that was in so much trouble with his ma a few years ago for wanting to go to school, Herman Taggert?" Her throat dried, remembering that terrible time. She asked carefully, "Is he still with the Currans?"

"Oh, yeah." Red laughed. "He's a straight up fella, an' a dang-good cowhand, the best the 7Cs got. He said to tell y'all howdy, especially you, Jocelyn, he thinks highly of you for helpin' him when you did."

"I'd do it again if I had to. He was a good boy who was treated plumb awful by his own mother. I'm so glad to hear that he's doing fine." She smiled in contentment. "Now then, unless someone else needs more dessert, I think we're finished here."

Nila quickly stacked the dishes while Jocelyn scraped pots and pans clean and filled the teakettle. The men left the table, still talking among themselves as they headed for the back door and the barn to finish up the last chores of the day. The moment they were gone, the women shared a look. Nila said, "We need to take milk to the two motherless calves and the water has to heat to wash the dishes so no need to stay in the kitchen."

Jocelyn added, "I need to see if that darned old Rhode Island Red hen has tried to make a nest in the barn again." She dried her hands on a dishtowel. *We're not about to miss any of the fascinating stories Red would still be telling as the men worked about the barn.* Grinning at each other as they left the house, Andy between them, each holding a hand, the three of them ran to catch up with the goings on in the barn. Her hens, scratching for worms in the barnyard, flew squawking from their path making Andy laugh with glee.

For the first few minutes at the barn, Jocelyn poked around in piles of sweet-smelling hay. Andy squatted each time to look, shaking his head when no eggs were found. They looked in dark corners of feed bins for signs of the hen's nesting efforts, with no luck. Satisfied, they joined Nila at her task, bottle feeding the calves born later than the usual spring season.

Their own chores completed, the trio drifted to where Rom was currying his mule, Shay, Pete and Red were shoveling stalls clean, readying them for spreading clean hay. Red was in the middle of a story about when the famous bulldogger, Bill Pickett, who the 101 Real West show billed as 'THE DUSKY DEMON', was still a young boy and got his beginning.

"Chousin' longhorn cattle outta them mesquite thickets in Texas wasn't no easy job for cowboys. Pickett was about ten years old when he got to watchin' bulldogs catch and hold cattle by snappin' on to the cow's lip with their teeth. Right then he deduced that if a bulldog could do that, so could a boy. He took to prac-ticin' catchin' an' holdin' stray calves thataway—bitin' onto the calf's lip an' throwin the critter down."

Nila made a face of distaste at Jocelyn, who gave her a half-grin in return and shrugged.

"Wasn't no time he was bulldoggin' beef cows and longhorns," Red was saying.

"Jumpin' off his horse onto a steer five times bigger than him, grabbin' the steer's horns, clampin' his teeth into the critter's lip while he dug his booted feet into the dirt and faster than lightnin' throws that steer down and ties him."

Rom, who'd gone to pitch hay from the loft, leaned down to ask, "Do they use that Bill Pickett fella reg'lar in the 101 Ranch Real West show?"

"Oh, yeah." Red looked up. He leaned on the pitchfork he was using. "Pickett rides his bay horse named Spradley in every show. Watchers get so excited seein' Pickett bulldog steers with his teeth that they practically jump outta their own skins. 'Hard and tough as whalebone' that's what they say about Bill Pickett. An' he is, I've seen him workin'."

For the next several minutes, Rom pitched hay furiously from the loft, then clambered back down the ladder and joined the men in adding it to the stalls to feed.

From her place seated on an upturned bucket, Jocelyn's mind began to wander. She'd read somewhere, probably in the *Skiddy Review* last year, about the first really huge gathering the Miller brothers drew to their equally big show. The brothers had gotten wind about the National Editorial Association convention to be held in Guthrie, Oklahoma. A side trip to the Millers Brothers' 101 Ranch was added to the convention's program. Editors and publishers from around the entire United States were thrilled to come to Bliss, Oklahoma, and see the 'wild and wooly west in action'. On their return, those newspaper editors' exciting stories about the event spread the word about the 101 Show to every town, large and small, in the country and beyond. 'Popularity of the 101 Ranch swelled to immeasurable proportions', papers said.

Her mind came back to what Red was telling the others. "They got that Indian, Geronimo, to be in the show, too. They plan to have him ridin' in a motorcar and shootin' from it at a buffalo, one'a those they have there on the 101 range."

"An Injun shooting a buffalo from a motor car?" Rom yelped. He burst into laughter. "I'd like to see that!"

"As if that's how it really happened in the old West," Jocelyn muttered. As much as she had enjoyed them, she had had enough, for the time being, of Red's stories about the 101 Ranch and its doings. The fact that Rom had swallowed every single tale tonight like it was cherry pie with cream would have been impossible to miss. She rose and headed for the door. Her heart sank as Red began a whole new story about the Millers Brothers' Trained Mules Act. Tears threatened behind her eyes. *Trained mules, even.* They'd lost their older boy, sure as anything. But it was his right to make his own choices, and she needed to step aside and let him be a man. A good man, like Pete.

Red bellowed, "Jocelyn, where ya goin'?"

"To finish up in the kitchen." She added, over the worry in her mind, "I liked the stories, Red. Thanks." She smiled over her shoulder and held her hand out to Andy who followed.

FIFTEEN

For the rest of the week, Red pitched in to help and did a large share of work cutting the last of the kaffir, moving cattle to fresh pasture, and tending odds and ends of chores Pete needed done on the Nickel Hill. On a hot summer evening, the whole family had taken to the porch where it was cooler. Off to the side, Rom plucked tunes on his banjo and Nila, laughing, played checkers more or less with Andy, using a homemade checkerboard and stones. In her rocker, Jocelyn worked at patching the elbows of Rom's favorite, nearly threadbare shirt. Seated on the steps, coffee cups in hand, Pete and Red engaged in an easy-going accounting of their accomplishments.

"I'm glad to hear all this, fellas, proud of you, too." Jocelyn managed to get a word in, accidentally pricking a finger with a needle in her hurry to do so. "Because now I need your help at the livery, not a big job—if you don't mind." Both Pete and Red turned to look at her, surprised. She explained. "One high wind after another this past spring loosened several stretches of the livery stable roof, or plumb blew it off in other places. It really needs fixing."

"Well, sure." Red scratched the side of his nose. "We can do that for the little lady, can't we, Pete?"

Pete hesitated. "Sure we can, I reckon we better get it done right soon, though. There's still some hayin' and barley and oats to harvest. Sorry, hon," he grinned at Jocelyn, "I saw the damage the wind did at the time, then somehow, forgot about it—with everything else going on."

"I understand, Pete, I know how busy we've all been." She quirked a grin at him.

"Sure have." He frowned and leaned his head back against the porch post. "I'll have to see what kinds of roofing Cochran's Hardware and lumber-yard keeps in stock."

Jocelyn's head came up, a shiver raced along her spine. She set her sewing aside. "Whatever you do, don't tell Cochran what the roofing is for. You might make out that it's for a shed here on the ranch, or something. The last thing on earth J.L. would want is for the livery to be improved on."

Red had a sudden puzzled look, listening to them.

"You're right, sweetheart. Fortunately, he probably won't be around. I doubt he knows a blamed thing about hardware and lumber, for sure he leaves any real work to be done to his manager." Pete went on to explain to Red about J.L. Cochran's efforts to end the livery for good, be replaced by a motorcar business.

Red wiped his moustache, threw back his head and roared with laughter. "The hell you say? Get rid of the only livery in Skiddy an' for miles around? The man ain't got no common sense."

"That's how I see it," Jocelyn murmured in quiet agreement. *None at all.*

~

"I'm so lucky to have your help on your days off, Nila, when I have matters to see to in Skiddy," Jocelyn said next morning as she settled her hat in place. "I was thinking that for supper you might make a meat pie? There's leftover beef roast and a little gravy in the icebox, and you can fry some onions and make more gravy with that. Mashed potatoes over the top of the meat. I like to moisten the top with milk, dot it with butter, and put it in the oven to brown."

Nila smiled. "With Andy's help, digging and washing the potatoes, we'll make a fine meat pie."

"Good." Jocelyn hugged Andy and headed outside where Pete and Red waited by the wagon. As they rumbled down the lane, headed for Skiddy and work at the livery, Jocelyn privately crossed her fingers in her skirts that the job with the roof could be completed without J.L. seeing and making trouble. Which he'd be hell-bent to do if he got wind of their plans.

The men had tied their horses to the back of the wagon—intending to return to the ranch if they finished early in town. Jocelyn found the clip-clopping of their horses' hooves, in back of her, a musical rhythm to the rattle of the wagon, a bright addition to the day.

~

"He wasn't there," Pete told Jocelyn as he and Red unloaded roofing from the wagon out back of the livery stable. "In fact, the hardware manager said J.L. was out of town on some business."

"Well, I'm glad for that." Jocelyn heaved a sigh of relief and turned her attention to helping unload for a short while. She watched Pete climb to the roof on the ladder they'd brought from the ranch, and Red passing roofing and nails up to him. Inside later, she visited with Prank, then tended to office chores.

Until late afternoon, the hammering and sounds of the men scrambling around on the roof continued. She took time to grocery shop at Noack's general store and, returning to the livery, was thinking that it was about time she headed for the ranch when the men came down declaring the repair job complete.

"Good. We'll all head for home and supper, then." She said to Red, "Nila is a good cook. You'll like her meat pie, and salad greens wilted with vinegar and sugar. She'll have iced tea ready, too. You two have surely earned it, and I thank you."

The men's eyes locked, their expressions showing mixed displeasure and debate. Pete drew a long breath. "We thought we'd go to the saloon for a bit, Jocey, honey. It was damn hot up there on the roof." He wiped his forehead on his sleeve and chin lifted, gave her a hopeful look.

Red had removed his purple neckerchief and was mopping his face with it. He grinned at Jocelyn. "I don't get to see your man here often and don't know when that might be again, once I take off back to Oklahoma and the 101. You don't mind our going for a little tangleleg now, do you?"

Jocelyn chewed her lip then mustered a smile as Pete stowed the ladder in the wagon and both men brushed themselves off. "I reckon it doesn't matter that much if you do. I couldn't be happier that those holes on the roof are taken care of, that Prank didn't climb up there to do it, like he'd told me he'd been fixing to do, and maybe fall and break some bones."

She whispered to Pete when he kissed her cheek, "Don't be out all night, please?" After they'd washed up a bit at the trough, she watched them head up the street in their usual rolling cowhand walk, happy as a pair of ganders off to a King's ten-acre pond. She cupped her mouth, intending to remind them that if they wanted breakfast at home, they knew when they'd better be there. Changing her mind, she dropped her hands and let them go. They were grown men, not children— which didn't mean, even so, that they'd employ good sense.

It was sometime after midnight that noise coming from outside stirred Jocelyn awake. A short while later, she could hear Pete's mumbling voice and Red's bellow followed by a deep chuckle. She felt relief that her man was home and hoped that they wouldn't wake the rest of the family. Curled against him later, breathing easy that all was well, she fell back to sleep.

~

"You didn't!" Jocelyn whispered fiercely to Pete next morning after he grabbed her arm and pulled her back into bed to 'get something off his chest'. She held her head in both hands then turned to look over at him. "You told Red that he could take Rom back to Oklahoma with him? How could you, Pete? The boy is too young, he would be under Red's influence, his care—and heaven help anybody in that shaky state of affairs." Her decision that Rom had a right to do what he wanted melted like ice in a hot skillet. She piled back onto her pillow, breathing short, fast breaths of fury, and deep disappointment.

"The boy wants this, Jocey. He's not exactly ours to order around and he's a good kid, smart, old enough to make up his own mind."

She rose on her elbow, and turned on him, spit flying. "Are you saying Rom has already decided, and he's leaving?" She wiped her mouth, knowing her question was useless.

"I'm sorry, honey, that what's done was kept from you, it ain't fair. But Rom has been getting ready on the sly for two or three days, to leave with Red. I didn't know until last night, when Red told me and I said it was okay, if this is what Rom wanted."

"Damn." She threw their blankets clean to the floor. "Damn everything!"

It was obvious at the breakfast table that both men were nursing hangovers, Pete looking embarrassed, Red short on appetite. Jocelyn was mad enough to crown them both with their breakfast. She watched Rom with a breaking heart. He was unnaturally quiet, his eyes on his plate in guilt seeing how upset she was, and trying at the same time to hide his excitement. Nila pretended with a solemn expression that nothing unusual was taking place. Little Andy was so absorbed in his puppy-shaped pancakes that Nila made for him to notice anything else. It was a most uncommon breakfast and the men rushed from the kitchen as soon as they had finished.

All the while Jocelyn cleaned her kitchen and made Rom's favorite raisin lemon pie, she was overcome by memories of the young boy—Rommy he was called, when he first came to them. His mother had died of consumption. Grieving, he and his pa, Chester Treyhern, left Nebraska to start over, in a new place, Kansas. They'd set up home in an abandoned shack a short way from the Nickel Hill Ranch. Unfortunately, Chester Treyhern couldn't find enough work to feed them, not an extra penny for anything.

Fighting starvation, Rom's father stole and butchered a steer from a neighboring ranch of thousands of acres, feeling sure that on a place with an almost identical number of cattle, one missing steer wouldn't be noticed. Threatened with hanging when it was found out, and accused of being the one stealing from all the ranchers around, Treyhern turned his son over to them and left for other parts. Rom, when he first came into Jocelyn and Pete's care, was a very sick boy with what was believed to be consumption—newly known as tuberculosis—his chances of surviving appeared to be small. As heaven would have it, he had a serious case of pneumonia, not tuberculosis, and with a doctor's care and Jocelyn's loving attention, he pulled through, to be the young man he was today.

More memories flooded her mind, slowing Jocelyn's movements as she dusted the front room furniture. She sat down and let the memories take over, elbows on her knees, chin in hand. Not too long ago, Rom's homely, decrepit old horse, Handsome, the boy's proudest possession and close comrade when he'd come to them, died. Luckily, her mule colt's—Shay's—playful companionship, helped the boy greatly through his loss of Handsome.

There was no doubt that Rommy was happy living with her and Pete from the start. Letters came now and then from his father, Chester Treyhern, a gaunt, mostly decent fellow, on the run from the possibility of being arrested for cattle theft. Rom read the short letters with some interest, but not once saying he wanted to be with his pa. In truth, until now, he'd made it clear he never wanted to leave Nickel Hill Ranch, leave his new family. Pete, Jocelyn, Nila and Andy. She wiped her eyes with her dust cloth, scowling and laughing when she realized the ridiculous thing she'd done.

Heavenly Hannah, I need to pull myself together. Even though Pete was hardly sober at the time he made up his mind, he was right that Rom should be allowed to make his own decisions. What would be, would be. Not that that eased the pain in her heart, or lessened her disappointment.

Later, in an effort to clear her moody feelings, Jocelyn hummed a few bars of My Old Kentucky Home as she carefully removed the baked raisin lemon pie from the oven, putting it by the window to cool. Breaking into song loud and clear, fully aware that she was not a good singer, she went to the icebox in their screened back porch, took out a chicken, caught and butchered the evening before, and took it to the kitchen to season before roasting in the oven. Out in the garden, still humming, with Andy's help, she picked fresh lettuce and onions for a salad, and dug new potatoes for making creamed new potatoes.

Looking out the kitchen window later, her eyes followed the hustle and bustle of Rom's last preparations to go with Red. She smiled, with effort, watching him carry the bench from the shade tree in the yard to the corral where later today he and his mule would perform for them one last time at Nickel Hill, before the two of them took off.

Red had left two or three of his horses with them when he first went down to Oklahoma and the 101 Ranch. They would be taking two of those along this time. The wilder horses were being shod, curried, and manes trimmed. Rom would ride Shay and lead one horse of Red's part of the time, then do the reverse other stretches. Red's mount would be the horse he'd come for, and he'd lead the one he'd ridden up from Oklahoma.

Jocelyn made an extra pan of biscuits so that she could send a batch with Rom and Red. She'd pack some ham and cold sliced beef, apples and boiled eggs for them to eat on the way, too. Andy was aware that Rom had promised to treat them all to Rom and Shay's Mule Trick Show before he left, and she could see Andy bouncing around at Rom's side as Rom lugged a square homemade wood platform into the corral, for Shay to stand on in the performance.

As directed by Rom when the time came, Jocelyn, Nila, and Andy sat on the provided bench. Pete and Red leaned against the corral gate, everyone ready to watch The Rom and Shay Mule Show, to take place in the center of the corral. First act was a simple trot around the inside of the corral, Rom, riding Shay, strumming his banjo and singing "*Coming Around the Mountain*". Their audience laughed at Shay braying right along, though not exactly in tune. At the finish, the whole family clapped and whooped.

Coming to a stop in the center of the corral, Rom dismounted, banjo strapped over his shoulder and willow wand in hand, to stand at the head of his mule, Shay wearing a rope of sunflowers around his neck. They turned to face their audience. "Are you glad to see these folks? If so, nod yes." Rom moved the willow wand in his hand but didn't use it to touch Shay at the throat as he had in weeks of training. "If so, nod yes." It was more a shake of the head, but Shay nodded and was awarded a treat of sliced carrot, and received more loud applause.

"Good mule!" Rom exclaimed petting and hugging Shay. "Now give me a kiss." Nothing. "Give me a kiss. You like me, don't you?" More rubbing. "Give me a kiss." Rom leaned in and Shay muzzled his cheek and the 'crowd' roared with laughter. Shay got another treat and a lot of loving pats.

Rom ground-reined his sunflower decorated mule and rolled a large barrel on its side into the center of the ring up to the square wood platform. Softly speaking encouragement, patting Shay's withers over and over in what seemed a long time, they then took off at a dust flying gallop around and around inside the circle, then headed back toward the barrel and platform to go sailing over both in a perfect jump. They trotted around to face the audience and receive their due—which was plenty.

After a few minutes Rom said, loud and clear, "The folks are very kind, aren't they, Shay? Give them a smile, Shay. Smiiile," he drew it out, smiiiile." Jocelyn remembered how Rom taught that trick. He would hold a treat in his left hand and say, "Smiiile" and with his right hand he'd pull Shay's lip up at the same time. It took days of trying, but finally Shay learned to smile just seeing the treat and told to "Smiiile." In fact, Shay often smiled just seeing Rom come toward him.

Andy clapped furiously. "Do it again, Rom, do it again, Shay!"

Twice more, Rom and Shay displayed their tricks to a happy 'crowd'. In their finale, they circled inside the corral, Rom vaulting off and on Shay's back, one side then the other, never slowing for a minute. When they stopped, Rom led Shay to the wood platform, the barrel rolled aside. He petted and praised Shay into climbing onto a square platform Then with a grand gesture, both Rom and mule bowed.

To all watching, it was clearly the best mule show on earth. And Jocelyn knew with certainty that there was no way she could stop Rom from his dream, nor did she want to, now.

The enjoyment of the day continued into the evening after supper and chores. Nila, confiding in Jocelyn that she could hardly bear the thought of Rom leaving, suggested they all join in on singing for the fun of it out on the porch where it was cooler. Leading the 'musicale' of old favorites in her beautiful voice, from *Oh! Susanna* to *Beautiful Dreamer* and *Gentle Annie*—"*When the springtime comes again gentle Annie*"—Nila encouraged the rest of them to join in.

Red, as it turned out, had a great singing voice, but boomed so loud in his Kansas drawl singing *CampTown Races* later—'*doo dah, doo dah*'—he drowned everyone else out. They all quieted to listen to Rom's banjo plunking and singing of a much improved 'Get Along Little Dogies'. And later, Red River Valley.

When he'd finished, Jocelyn caught Pete's eye on her. He winked and pulled his harmonica from a pocket. She lay a hand over her heart and smiled. Like the painting he used to do before they married, he hardly ever played his mouth harp. In fact, she didn't know that he had one until she'd found it in the pocket of an old coat that he'd worn in his cowboying days. A time, she supposed, when he made music with other cowhands around a campfire. Eyes on her, he brought the harmonica to his mouth, tested it a little, then began to play the beautiful notes of Oh, Shenandoah, one of her favorite songs. Her heart sang "I hear you calling... I'm bound away 'cross the wide Missouri." One by one, the others picked up on the song, singing what they knew of it. Jocelyn didn't think she'd ever had a better evening, for any reason, any time.

Until little Andy, perturbed, asked to sing a song by himself. The family agreed, one and all.

"How about 'I'm a Little Teapot'?" Nila suggested. He made a face and shook his head. "Aright then, what about, 'I Know an Old Lady Who Swallowed a Fly'?"

He stood up, beaming, and sang, "...I don't know why she swallowed a flyyyy. The old lady swallowed a spider—that wriggled and jiggled insiiide herrrr." He doubled over and burst into laughter at his own song.

Nila hugged him, laughing, when he finished, his shoulders back and wearing a wide grin of pride. "I'll sing Doo Dah now," he offered.

"No, I think we've Doo Dahed enough for tonight." Pete stood, harmonica in hand. "Time for bed. But you sang mighty fine, Son."

"Yes, Andy, you're a good singer." Jocelyn gave him a hug and took his hand to lead him upstairs to bed.

"Pretty durn good, I got to say." Rom gave Andy a pat on the head as he walked by.

"Good like your mule show, wasn't I?" Andy asked earnestly, and waited.

Churring crickets in the descending dark filled a full minute of silence.

Rom started to say something then stopped, gulped. A stricken look came into his eyes that had nothing to do with singing or mules. Color flooded his face and he chewed his lip. Then he recovered and said, "Sure was, fella."

Her older boy had just realized, Jocelyn guessed, that day to day enjoyment of life with Andy and with the rest of them, was about to end. *From this valley they say you are going...* Unfortunately, he'd probably not been struck hard enough to change his mind.

SIXTEEN

The entire family was up before dawn the next day to see Rom and Red off on their way to Oklahoma. Determined to make the best of Rom's leaving, Jocelyn forced a smile and gave him the food she'd packed to put in his saddlebag. "I'm not sure you're going anywhere with Red is a good idea," she said in an undertone. "He's a good man mostly, but he's got bad habits I'd rather you didn't take on for yourself." She gave him a pointed, questioning look.

Rom, hat in hand, banjo strapped over his shoulder, shook his head. "I won't, Ma."

"I hope this 101 Ranch Real West Show is what you're looking for, and I reckon it is—and it'll make you a happy life. But if it doesn't, you come right on back home, here. We...love you, Son. Remember that, wherever you are." She swiped at a tear under her eye.

"I'll never forget you all, that's for certain." He blew out a long breath and smiled. "And even if I do like what I find down in Oklahoma, it ain't so far that I can't come home for visits."

"You do that!" Her spirits picked up. "I'll write you letters, Rom, and you write back, please, all about your doings down there."

"I will, Ma." He hesitated, his Adam's apple bobbing in his throat. "I can't ever thank you enough for givin' me a home when I may have died, if you hadn't. I had that rotten pneumonia. My pa, besides needin' to get away from them that wanted to hang him for somethin' he didn't do, didn't have the money to take me to a doctor. You saved my life, Ma, and that part I ain't never forgettin'."

She grabbed him in a hard hug and then shoved him toward his horse. "You two are wasting daylight, better get going."

Pete came to put his arm around her waist.

Nila, tears in her eyes, picked up Andy and the two waved over and over.

The four of them watched until Rom and Red were ant-dots on the road, before turning to daily doings that would take their hearts to a happier place.

It had been a few days since Jocelyn had been to Skiddy to check on matters at the livery and she was anxious to be there on this bright sunny morning. She snapped the reins over Alice and Zenith and sat high in the wagon. "C'mon, mules, we've got work to do, no lagging." They took the cue and swung into a faster trot. She worried about Prank managing the business by himself, without Rom to help when he needed it. Hiring a replacement was the answer, but who? She'd like to be the one, but that was near impossible with all she had to do at home on the ranch and caring for Andy. This being near harvest time especially, with all the canning and preserving she needed to do. And more. One thing she knew for sure, fretting about it fixed nothing.

"Now don't you worry yourself none, missus," Prank said, after she'd reached the livery and he'd heard her out. "Ol' Homer Tuttle, you know who he is, an ol' feller like me but still has enough 'get up and go' to help here. He hangs around the livery fair regular, anyhow, and many a time he's helped me when I needed it. Iffen' you want to take him on steady, I know dinged well he'll do it. No need to pay 'im, cash money, but if you want to give Homer eggs an' garden sass now and then, I know it'd please 'im."

"Really? I could pay him some, and I definitely have eggs, fruit and vegetables extra for him."

"Good. I purt near hired him a'ready, anyhow." He grinned sheepishly. "He was here first thing this morning, but Homer went home to feed his dog and put some soup on the stove for our dinner."

She smiled and patted his shoulder. "Bless you both, that's at least one worry off my mind today." For the next hour, she went over paperwork in the livery office, the cubbyhole beyond the stalls warm and stuffy this morning. It was a relief, later, to head to Noack's store for groceries needed at the ranch. When she saw through the window that J.L. Cochran was there, talking to Elsa, she stopped and almost reversed her way. Her stomach churning, she entered.

J. L. held his hat in one hand, and gestured wide with his cigar in the other, sending a twinkle of sparks to the floor. "A fine business woman that you are, Mrs.

Noack, I know you'll want to back my cause for the sake of Skiddy's future. For the benefit of all our citizens, for every person in the county, matter of fact. We count on you and all other dear women of the town, to do what's right."

What was 'right' to him? Jocelyn wondered.

Elsa grimaced, came from behind the counter, and stepped on the ash of his cigar although the sparks looked to be out. She waved off his words like she was swatting a pesky fly. "You mean, with the town election coming soon and the fact that women are now allowed to vote in town matters—if not federal elections as yet— you want me to agree with your foolish plan to get rid of the livery? You expect every woman in town to bow down to your wishes? Along with the men to support you?" Elsa cocked her head, her eyes darkened with disdain.

"I do, damn it," he blustered, his neck growing red. "What I'm suggesting is desperately needed if the town is to ever show any progress." He leaned forward, chomping his cigar, fingers flexing, as if wanting to pound his opinion into her.

"Progress is a fine new horse available for renting at the livery, or a buggy newly painted. Wouldn't you see it that way, Jocelyn?" Elsa smiled over J.L.'s shoulder at Jocelyn.

"That's progress absolutely." Jocelyn stepped forward, grocery list in hand. "If it isn't a bother—" she all but shoved J.L. out of her way, "I need to buy my groceries and head on back to the ranch."

"You're going to be sorry, both of you women and your friends, if you don't come to your senses, soon." Sweat blossomed on Cochran's forehead, he clapped his hat on, glared at the two of them with a look that laid them out dead on the floor, and turned to go.

"Mr. Cochran," Jocelyn called after him, "if you don't like the way we do things in Skiddy, shouldn't you find another town where they'd agree with what you're wanting?" *Little chance of that.*

He looked long and hard at her, his expression finally altering to his fake, slimy smile. He huffed, "I'm here to stay." And slammed the door as he left the store.

"That man is beginning to scare me." Elsa bit her lip, and blew out short breaths. "Hate is growing like a weed day by day inside J.L. Cochran, it seems to me."

"I see it, too." Jocelyn rubbed at the chill bumps on her arms. "I'd give anything if he'd recognize that he's finished here in Skiddy, and just go." *Or, if Marshal Hillis and other law officers were going to arrest J.L. for his past crimes, that they'd get on with it.*

~

I n a far better mood a couple days later, Jocelyn strolled their lane to the crossroad, and opened the mailbox. "What?" she said out loud, yanking at the envelope inside. "What!?"

It had been a very long time since she'd had a letter from Nila's mother, Flaudie Malone. Who at one time had been a terrible pest writing letters—having convinced herself that Jocelyn's Grandma Letty, who was her Aunt Letty, had left things of value when she died, including Nickel Hill Ranch. She'd repeatedly blamed Jocelyn for 'taking it all'. Not sharing a thing. After explaining matters very clearly in a letter to Flaudie that poor Gram had next to nothing to leave, and they were just managers of the ranch, the letters had ended. Flaudie's final act was to throw her daughter Nila out after a disagreement, send her to Jocelyn and Pete to care for, as Gram had taken in Jocelyn. The difference, Jocelyn was a newborn baby, Nila was a fifteen-year-old, a sweet girl with a mind of her own and nothing like her mother, Flaudie. *Thank Hannah.* Biting her lip, her muscles tense, she tore the letter open and began to read.

In the house, Jocelyn dropped into a chair, disbelieving that this strange woman could be doing this. She scratched her cheek and read the letter again:

Dear Mrs. Pladson,

> *This is to let you know that I'm comin' in person to see Aunt Letty's ranch that you live on for myself. I've thought about this a long time, and I've come to believe that you made up lies about Aunt Letty leavin' nothin' for me. You invented the reason you and your husband came to be runnin' the place that once was hers. I doubt that my daughter, Nila, still lives with you, that she's moved on. In that case, be at the Skiddy train station September 10th to pick me up. Nila's Pa died two weeks ago. Left me in terrible debt. I'm comin' for what is due me. We're goin' to have this out once and for all, so be prepared!*

> *Flaudie Malone*

With hands to her aching temples, Jocelyn went to the window and looked at Nila, digging potatoes in the garden, Andy picking them up and putting them in a bucket. How could such a smart, sweet person, be the daughter of a woman like Flaudie? They were as different as sauerkraut was to peach ice cream. *Blast the woman!*

Nila cried a short time later when she read the letter. Not about her mother on her way to Skiddy, but her father's passing. "My papa was the nicest person on earth, Jocelyn. Gentle and kind to everybody. Worked so hard on our farm. I should have stayed and helped, made his life easier because I can believe that my ma harassed him into his grave. Nothing he did ever suited her, no matter how hard he tried. Or I tried." She was silent a moment, wiping her eyes. "If you don't have a need for the team and wagon tomorrow, I will take it and pick her up myself, have a long talk with her on the way back from town. I'm not going to allow her to brow-beat me like she always did before, calling me names because I didn't marry the old gent she picked for me to marry. What she wanted out of that, was his money. No concern for how I felt about it whatsoever."

"I'm sorry, Nila. Andy and I could come with you to pick your mother up, if it would help."

"No. Thank you. I need to talk to her alone. Maybe I can talk her into getting back on the train."

"If that's what you want." Deep in her apron pocket, Jocelyn crossed her fingers.

Hours passed while Jocelyn finished canning corn and snap beans. Andy, after his nap, played with toy animals, putting on a pretend show much like the Rom and Shay's Mule Show. It was almost dark, the sun going down, when Nila drove the team and wagon to a stop in front of the house. Jocelyn licked her lip feeling cautious hope. She went out onto the porch to greet them, feeling fidgety as Nila helped her mother, a small, wiry woman in a yellow flowered dress and dark blue slat bonnet, from the wagon.

Jocelyn held out her hand as Flaudie came up the steps. "Hello, Mrs. Malone. I'm Jocelyn. Come on inside."

"I wish to the Lord so," she said in a flat tone. "It's been a hellish trip out here, not to mention how late I had to set and wait for someone to pick me up."

Jocelyn looked at Nila, who explained. "A mule had got out somehow and was making his way here and there around town, through gardens, scaring some little children, ripping through clothes that were hanging from clothes lines. I helped Prank track the mule down and bring it back to the livery. I was late to the train."

"I'll say, late," her mother exclaimed. She removed her bonnet, exposing dark hair damp with perspiration and starting to grey, and wound in a large knot in back. "And with a name like 'Prank' I'd suspect that person guilty of letting the mule run loose."

"Not his fault, Ma. Prank operates the Skiddy livery stable. He'd for sure not let a mule run off."

"Maybe he did and couldn't help it," Flaudie said, wanting to win.

"Please, let's go inside to supper. If you'd like to freshen up, I've heated a teakettle of water and we can add it to the pump water here on the porch." Jocelyn pointed to a washstand holding a basin and soap dish, towels hanging to the side, and a mirror on the wall above.

"I'm starved, after waiting for so long. I'd rather just go eat." She looked at her hands, nodded, and marched ahead of the others into the house.

Considering that they would have a guest, Jocelyn had fixed a special supper. Roast pork and gravy, new potatoes 'in their jackets', fresh cooked green beans, hot rolls and rhubarb jam, and a mulberry pie for dessert. Their guest ate heartily, but announced that although the roast pork was so so, she'd tasted boiled possum that was better.

Pete choked on his pie, trying not to laugh out loud. Jocelyn's face heated in anger. Nila looked at her mother with something very close to disgust edging on a wish to kill. Andy piped up, "I like the pie real lots. Can I have some more, Momma?"

Jocelyn was about to turn him down when Flaudie said, "Why, the little pig!"

"Yes, you can, Son." Jocelyn sliced another piece and slapped it on his plate. She looked at Flaudie and from the deepest depths of her being brought up the closest she could come to a genuine smile.

While Jocelyn and Nila washed the supper dishes and tidied up the kitchen, Flaudie sat at the kitchen table making odd noises in her throat, patting her foot sharply on the floor, waiting for Jocelyn to prove the property that had belonged to Aunt Letty, and taken by Jocelyn and her husband on Letty's death, was really meant to be Flaudie's. Over in the corner Pete waited, due to Jocelyn's request that they both be present when Flaudie Malone was shown Francina Gorham's will, their dear friend legally having left Nickel Hill to Jocelyn and Pete on Francina's death.

Jocelyn hung the damp dish towels to dry, wishing to roll one into a twist and put it around the woman's throat. Still, she managed to smile. "I don't see why this is necessary but..."

"Don't stall, or lie to me. I'm positive you took this place from Aunt Letty's will, and in that way, from me. If you have proof of what you say, show it." Her face looked triumphant with disbelief.

"Ma," Nila protested, "Mrs. Pladson is telling the pure truth. You have no right to accuse her of lying. Nickel Hill is the Pladson ranch, fair and square, I have no doubt of it."

"But you don't know for sure, girl, do you?"

Nila gave her mother a scathing look, reached for Andy's hand, and said, "Let's play outside for a while." Andy took her hand and skipped alongside as Nila strode to the kitchen door and yanked it open hard.

Jocelyn stared. In all this time, she'd never seen Nila angry. And she could fully understand why. This woman could get under an angel's skin. Easily.

Flaudie stared at the papers Jocelyn spread before her so long that Jocelyn began to think she couldn't read. She was mouthing, sounding out, every word. She finally looked at Jocelyn and asked, "Who is Francina Gorham?"

"A very dear friend of ours. We managed Nickel Hill for her, the owner. From the beginning, she wanted us to have Nickel Hill Ranch when she passed."

"Who is Whitman Hanley?"

"Mrs. Gorham's son and my boss and friend when I helped with a mule drive. He was later killed by outlaws."

"How can he be her son? Their last names ain't the same."

"Whit Hanley had a step-father, Mr. Gorham."

"This other name, down here at the bottom?"

Flaudie cocked her head, sour disbelief in her face at everything Jocelyn had stated.

Pete was struggling so hard not to laugh that Jocelyn had to kick him under the table.

"That would be Mrs. Gorham's lawyer. The other four names you see and kind of skipped over are two witnesses to the legality of the will and above that— Pete, and me, named legal owners of Nickel Hill Ranch."

Flaudie was silent for several minutes. She scratched her arm. "Is there a place for me to sleep? I'm plumb wore out."

"I'll show you. Come." Jocelyn jumped to her feet and motioned. Another cot had been placed in the screened porch that was Nila's room. Jocelyn stood back and waited. "The cot over here." She fluffed the pillow.

"I suppose this is Nila's room." She looked around. "I recognize some of her things." She added in a tart tone, "Reckon I'll sleep here, if you don't have a room alone for me?" She plopped her satchel on the floor and looked at Jocelyn accusingly.

Jocelyn pressed her lips together, prayed for patience, and shook her head. "Sorry, but no. We have a good-sized family, and a house short on bedrooms."

The next week stretched Jocelyn's patience to the raw brink of toleration. Flaudie Malone complained about some part of a meal each and every day, as though she'd been appointed to criticize. She corrected Andy on any little thing she fathomed wrong, not waiting for Jocelyn or Pete to do so, if it was needed. Pete's moustache was not proper for his face, Jocelyn wore her hair too uppity for a country woman and she didn't hang her sheets right on the clothesline.

One day Flaudie came in from sitting on the porch and thumbing over her shoulder, said, "There's a fella just rode in, looks like a saddle bum to me. Want I should run him off?"

"Wait a minute, Flaudie." Jocelyn turned and held up her hand from where she'd been peeling potatoes. "I'll see who it is, might be a neighbor." She went to the door and looked out. "Oh, my goodness, it's Rom, our older boy." She pressed her hands to her mouth. *Was it really Rom? Why had he come back?* A thousand currents of joy went through her as Jocelyn raced across the porch, down the steps, to where Rom was swinging down out of the saddle, and Shay brayed a greeting.

SEVENTEEN

"What happened, why are you here, Rom?"
She flung her arms around him, ignoring
that he was covered with dust and smelled
strongly of horse and sweat. "I don't think I could be
more tickled to see you." She took Shay's lines from him
and briefly eyed Flaudie waiting expectantly on the
porch. "We can talk down at the barn, and take care of
this mule and your horse." They stopped on the way for
Rom to drink three dippers full of cold water at the
well, take his hat off and splash more water on his
sweaty head. Jocelyn watched, caring so much that he
was here but wondering. Did the 101 Ranch folks not
want him, and turned him away? If so, they were fools.

He took off walking, chickens clucking and flapping
from his path. He nodded tiredly at the horse and his
mule. "Let's take care of these critters and then I'll tell
you how come I'm back."

"Now then," Jocelyn said when the animals had
been given feed and water. "What happened?" She

took a seat on an old wood storage box holding horse-shoes, nails and such.

Stroking Shay's neck, Rom looked over at her, "Red's fine stories that he told us all was probably true, but none of that is what he's doin' down there on the 101. Come to find out, I'd probably be shovelin' horse dung and punchin' cows, breakin' horses when needed, the same as his job there now."

Jocelyn rubbed her brow. "That fiddle-footed man. Why am I not surprised?"

"Yeh. He figured in time they'd let me be a rider in the show, or me and Shay doin' our tricks but I'd have to work up to it. The bosses runnin' the place was gone on a tour with the 101 Ranch Real West Show and not there for me to talk to anyway, so I come back." He gave her face a long study. "I never should'a gone with Red in the first place. Shouldn't a' left you and Prank high and dry. I'm plumb sorry, Ma."

"Now you don't need to worry about none of that." She frowned and waved her hand. "I wanted you to have your dream near as much as you did. You were led to expect different than you found, that's not your doing. How did Red feel about your coming back here to your folks?" *Not that it matters a trifle to me one way or another. I'm thankful that you're home safe and that's all.*

"Not much he could say. I told him I could shovel horse dung and punch cattle right here like I'd been doin', with my family."

"I'm pure sorry things didn't turn out how you hoped they would, Rom." She watched his face, hoping he'd get over his disappointment soon.

"No need to be sorry, Ma. I feel awful good just bein' back here." He wore a satisfied grin. "Someday, though, I'm goin' to make another trip down to Oklahoma and the 101 Ranch. When I'm more ready to hire on. I told Red that's what I'd do, and thanked him for letting me know a lot about the 101."

She smiled at him. "You will, yes. And I'll be watching you perform in that fancy 101 Real West Show. I just know it."

"Who is that woman on the porch?" Rom asked as they headed back toward the house.

Jocelyn hesitated, touched his arm. "Oh, my. She's Nila's mother come to visit. Her name is Flaudie Malone and she's a provoker beyond all measure. Nothing whatsoever is the woman like Nila. I'm not sure how much longer I can put up with her. Somehow, I need a way to send her back to Missouri where she came from, a nice way that she'll like, and won't hold it against me."

He patted her shoulder and grinned. "You'll do it, Ma. Bettin' on ya."

She shrugged, "I don't know, Son, I don't know." *A pest of any kind can sometimes be so blessed hard to be rid of, such as J.L. "Cockroach" Cochran.*

That night after supper, the whole family sat out on the porch where it wasn't as hot. Nila and Andy close on either side of Rom, glad to see their brother home again. Knowing the only way to keep Flaudie from dragging up another list of faults none of the Pladson family knew they had, Jocelyn told stories about Grandma Letty, Flaudie's Aunt Letty. The old stories one of the few things that'd keep the woman somewhat happy and silent.

She told them about Kansas City, Missouri, the little grey rented shack in the Kaw River bottoms where she and Grandma Letty lived. The smelly close-by stockyards and smoky, odorous rendering plants that were probably what made Grandma Letty bad sick. How, at age twelve, she took over Grandma Letty's laundry business, her grandmother no longer able. She drove the cart used to pick up and deliver folks' laundry. The beloved brown horse that pulled the cart was named Napoleon. For short, Jocelyn called him Nappy, or Nap. She told stories about their hen, Opal, and their rooster named Don Juan.

"It was happy news, when a letter came from a Kansas lawyer telling about a small farm in the Neosho River Valley in Kansas, that my Pa owned but had abandoned. That my name was on the deed, too. Papa, who was a teacher, by the way, was torn up by sorrow when his young wife, my mother, died. He'd turned to drifting, left me, just a baby then, for Grandma Letty to raise. In short order, I darn well knew what I wanted to do, the biggest decision I ever made in my twelve years of life. I wrote to the lawyer telling him that me and Grandma Letty was coming to take over the little farm."

"You were just a child," Nila said in awe. Others in the family nodded.

"Had to grow up fast. Life was so much better for the two of us on that farm, even if I had to do most of the work. Grandma Letty had come to like being abed and waited on, even as her sickness was healing. It was there on that farm," she licked her lip, "that two traveling sewing machine salesmen told Gram and me about surgery that could be done for—for my—my cleft lip." She was silent for a minute or two, as were her listeners. Pete was grinning, wiping moisture from his eyes on the back of his hand. She smiled back at him, he was fifteen years old when they'd met on that farm, his family being neighbors. Luckily, they'd met again ten years later under different circumstances.

She continued, "Papa, home from traipsing around down in Mexico and who knows where else, found me in that hospital on the hill, in Kansas City, with my mouth repaired." She swallowed and smiled. "A wondrous day for us both. Gram, too."

Jocelyn looked around at her dear family, and at Nila's mother. They were all looking back at her as though she were a living fairy tale, dropped into their lives. One by one, except Flaudie, hugged her. Sitting up straight, filled with contentment, she told them, "That moon out there is pretty high in the sky, we should all go to bed." She picked up the lamp on the small table by her chair, and shooed them one by one, inside.

～

The stories about Grandma Letty softened Flaudie's manner a little, but she still found much to complain about. No room of her own, no privacy. Andy, too noisy when he was inside the house and he should be made to stay outside, more. Nila 'paid more attention to the Pladson family than she had ever paid to her', the ungrateful girl.

More than once, Jocelyn was very close to leading the woman to the door and pointing to the road. And would have, likely, if she hadn't been able to escape to

Skiddy and the livery, taking Andy with her. Trips into the surrounding countryside to buy or sell mules, or just talk about mules, was most pleasant, a life saver.

She was home the day she looked up from the clothesline to see a fancy buggy drawn by a sleek bay horse coming up their lane. Hanging her clothespin bag on the line, removing her apron, and brushing her hair into place, she waited to see who it was. The stranger was tall, and well-dressed from grey fedora to a finely cut suit and blue tie, shining boots. He wore a thick but well-trimmed beard, and a full moustache.

He tipped his hat to her. "Good day, ma'am. You are Mrs. Pladson?"

"I am. Can I help you?"

He held out his hand, and shook hers. "My name is David Clark. Your neighbor, Mrs. Goody, told me you might have interest in what I have to offer." He reached into the buggy and pulled out a flat, shining leather case. "May I show you?" He motioned toward the house.

Feeling somewhat leery, she led him up the porch steps and into the front room. "Have a chair, Mr. Clark." *In the name of Hannah, what would he have in his fancy case that I'd take to?*

He sat down, waited for her to sit in the chair close by. Flaudie, evidently awakened from her nap, slipped into the room and another chair, stretching her neck to see. The gentleman put down the case and crossed to take her hand and introduce himself. "David Clark, and you?" Flaudie's face turned rosy. Her chest thrown out and ankles neatly crossed, she gave him her hand. "I'm Flaudie Malone."

Jocelyn stared open-mouthed at the transformation in the woman for a second or two, then returned her attention to the gentleman, who she now surmised was a traveling salesman. Likely selling something she didn't need or that she would like but couldn't afford. He opened the case and held it to show the contents. Jocelyn gasped. The most beautiful silverware she'd ever laid eyes on glittered back at her.

"This is the finest solid silver tableware that money can buy, and in two beautiful patterns as you can see." He showed them, giving them time to admire the spoons, forks, the serving spoons, the butter knives. "A set for twelve people is most affordable, and the company I work for accepts monthly payments—you don't need to pay the whole amount at once. Just five dollars a month would be all until the full fifty dollars is met."

He rushed on before Jocelyn could say anything. "You have children, I take it? There are few things as grand as this silverware to hand down in a family. Generation to generation, it would be a priceless treasure."

"Right after coming into owning family land you always counted on." Flaudie, butting in, sparkled at the salesman.

Jocelyn looked at her, swallowed what she'd like to reply, and turned to the salesman. "Mr. Clark, should I ever sell the livery stable that I own, I'd buy your silverware. Right now, I just cannot afford to buy it, as much as I'd like to. I'm sorry to have wasted your time."

He didn't look as disappointed or upset with her answer as she would have expected. Mr. Clark looked at Flaudie, who gaped and smiled from across the room.

"Mrs. Malone, I'd like to have a few words in private with Mrs. Pladson, if you don't mind." His glance went to the door.

Her face fell, but she stood and left the room, swishing her long skirts as she went.

How peculiar, Jocelyn thought, smiling to herself.

"You don't recognize me, do you, Mrs. Pladson?" Clark asked when the door had closed.

"I don't know what you mean. I'm sure I've never seen you before, Mr. Clark."

"You have seen me, Mrs. Jocelyn Royal Pladson." He sat forward in his chair, giving her a closer look at his face. He leaned back and smiled. "I'm Chester Treyhern. I'm here to see my son, Rommy Treyhern."

She was shocked, confused, her heart thudded. "You can't be Chester Treyhern." *The ragged farmer from Nebraska? Cattle thief who stole a steer to ward off starvation, who lived with Rom in an abandoned shack, who barely escaped the noose thanks to Pete and me? He couldn't be, could he?*

"I am. I'm sorry to take you by surprise, Mrs. Pladson, but I am Chester Treyhern, Rommy's father." He sat straighter. "In Denver, I took a salesman's class, learned all the good tricks of selling, being a salesman. I made myself over to what you see, and I've been very successful in the trade I've chosen. I'd like some time with Rommy, is he here?"

"Not now, no. He's in Skiddy helping out at my livery stable." She was still too stunned for more words, opened her mouth, closed it. She was beginning to see a resemblance to Rom's father. Without the heavy beard, the fancy moustache, and greying hair, yes, she could see that he could be an older and obviously wiser, Chester Treyhern.

He stood, again took her hand. "I'll see him there then, hopefully in private. I've already taken a hotel room in Skiddy, with the intention of seeing my boy. Thank you so much, Mrs. Pladson. For giving me your time today. I'm indebted to you and your husband forever for the money you gave me back then, so that I could get out of town before drunk cowboys could 'string me up' in the nearest cottonwood. Especially for taking good care of my son for so long. If he's ready to go with me, I have more to offer these days, and I'm ready to be a decent father."

A few minutes later, she escorted him to the door and watched him leave, Flaudie standing close behind her. "Hmm," was all Jocelyn had to say, finding it hard to believe what had just happened. And yet, in her heart, she knew that he'd told the truth, he was Chester Treyhern.

"What'd he talk to you about, Mrs. Pladson, something besides the silverware?"

"Nothing important, really. Just a simple, private conversation."

At supper, the silverware salesman was the chief topic of conversation. Jocelyn right away had taken Pete aside, and to his shock, convinced him that the man David Clark was actually Chester Treyhern. Made the point strongly that they keep the secret to themselves as to who he really was, except for Rom. They were to know him only as a traveling salesman. She smiled around at the family, and Flaudie. "Solid silver, the utensils were so beautiful. As much as I'd love to have them, I can't imagine when I'd use them. They are so fine."

"Is Mr. Clark coming back?" Flaudie asked later in the conversation with a hopeful giggle.

"Not that I know of," Jocelyn answered. "From what he said, he's staying at the hotel in Skiddy, I have no idea for how long before Mr. Clark will be back on the road, selling again."

"Skiddy, that dumpy little town, has a hotel?" Flaudie sat up straighter and slapped her palm on the table. "By-cripes, why am I not there? What's the hotel like?"

"The hotel is very nice," Nila answered. "I work at the hotel, serving in the dining room, during the summer when I'm not teaching."

"Well, for heaven's sake, get me a room there. Like you should've done already. You work, you must have money. You can do that much for me, your own mother, can't you?"

Nila spilled tea as she set her glass down. It took a while, but she said, "Yes, Ma, I'm sorry, I should have done that—if it's what you wanted. I'll do what I can to get you a hotel room in Skiddy."

"First thing in the morning, I'll be ready and you be ready, too."

"But—tomorrow I'm supposed to be here with Andy, so that Jocelyn can make a long drive to see some mules that's for sale."

Flaudie flipped her hand in dismissal. "That can be put off."

Jocelyn bit back what she wanted to say and forced a smile of agreement. She looked at Nila, knew the young woman so well by now that she could read her expression, her deep disappointment. *"There goes my savings meant for the learning I need, to be the journalist I so want to be. My life."*

This was not fair, not fair, even as badly as Jocelyn would like to see Flaudie Malone gone from the ranch.

EIGHTEEN

Home at last. Jocelyn patted Andy's small body curled up beside her on the wagon seat, drove the lane and drew the team to a halt in front of the house. She let her head fall back in weary relief. Nila charged out the front door and seeing Andy asleep, she stopped and said softly, "You took the young'un with you?" She frowned, rubbing at her forehead. "I'm sorry my Mama made you do that. She can be so rude, sometimes. It's always been that way. You go ahead and take Andy inside. Let me take your team to the barn. Supper's ready on the stove."

Jocelyn climbed down, waited for her wobbly legs to come to life, and gathered Andy in her arms. "He didn't go with me, Nila. Sometimes he likes to go on the drives, but other times, like today, he asks to stay with Mabel Goody. I just picked him up from Mabel's house, he fell asleep on the way here."

Nila looked relieved as she climbed into Jocelyn's place in the wagon and took up the lines, choosing to drive up the hill to the barns and pens rather than walking the mules. "Even so," she said over her shoulder as she began to move away, "Ma had no right to treat you and your family how she did."

Jocelyn lifted her right shoulder, the other one occupied by Andy's sleepy head, and smiled. *One good thing, Flaudie wanted to be in Skiddy, not here.*

Later that evening, redding up the kitchen together, Nila hung a fresh dish towel on the hook and said to Jocelyn, who busily pushed chairs closer in to the table, "I paid the hotel two week's rent for Ma. You've got no idea how much I wanted to take the key and lock her inside."

Jocelyn pressed her lips against a shocked laugh.

"She might be my real mother, but she gets my dander up bad—about as close to Kansas's thunder and lightning as a body can feel."

"Was she satisfied with the hotel, happy about it?" Jocelyn placed a small bouquet of purple asters back in the center of the clean table.

"Oh, yes. If she stays on for very long," Nila's hands clenched and her face filled with a look of disappointment, "my saved money will be gone in no time."

She went to stare out the window, to hide her frustration, Jocelyn guessed.

"If it comes to that, Nila, Pete and I intend to help you pay for your education."

"No." She turned, "I want to do that myself, pay my own way. I'll figure out something." She rubbed her arms. "I'm going to give Ma a little time, and if she decides to stay on in Skiddy, I'm going to suggest she get a job. Maybe in the hotel, cooking, or in the laundry room. Something. At one of the stores, maybe." She looked at Jocelyn with a half-smile and her voice rose,

"When we got to the hotel, we saw Mr. Clark, the salesman, in the lobby. Ma got plumb giddy seeing him, chatted away with Mr. Clark like if she was a girl my age. He invited her to have dinner with him at the hotel. Can you imagine that?" She hesitated. "He was awful nice to her, so maybe she won't bother him as much as she does most folks."

"Hmmm." Jocelyn couldn't contain her wide smile.
'What?"

"Nothing, really. Oh well, I suppose I can share my passing thoughts. What if those two, your mother and 'David Clark' actually like one another, enjoy one another's company, took to one another permanent?" She added quickly, "Did he say how long he'd be there, in Skiddy?" *He wanted to see Rom. She'd be surprised if Rom decided to go back with his father, and should he not agree to, Mr. Clark would likely stick around for a long visit at the very least.*

"He did mention it, and said he'd be staying there at the hotel for a couple more weeks, maybe longer. I overheard him telling Ma he's been making sales calls about his silverware, driving as far as Council Grove and other towns, but his best sales had always been in large cities. He plans to move on next to Topeka, and Kansas City. Maybe down south to those rich plantations—he said that he looks forward to doing that someday." Nila clasped her palms together at her chin and her eyes twinkled. "But you don't think, really, that Ma and Mr. Clark...?"

"You never know about some people," Jocelyn mused with a crooked grin, "the oddest couples do fall in love, have no trouble making a happy life. Happens all the time."

Nila's shoulders dropped, and she heaved a heavy sigh. "If she treats Mr. Clark like she bullied my poor Pa, it'll never happen."

"That's possible, too, I reckon. Let's hope that fate steps in and makes the right things, good things, happen."

~

I n the meantime, Jocelyn concluded, other, more serious matters needed tending. On a trip to have a look at mules that a rancher had for sale—they weren't quite what she was looking for in mules at present as it turned out—she'd eagerly used her time on the road to visit folks on a ranch she came upon, a couple of farms, and several families living closer to Skiddy. Over and over in discussions that followed, she brought up the upcoming election, asking friends to vote for George Jacobsen, owner of the feed store, to fill the council vacancy left by Mrs. Elsa Noack, co-owner of the Skiddy general store. Most folks knew George as a good man, a person inclined to want the best for most everyone. Were aware that he realized the same as Jocelyn did, that getting rid of the livery and replacing it with high-cost motorcars might be a good idea, someday, but this was a time too early for such a drastic move. The person to avoid voting for was J.L. Cochran, the newcomer behind the plan to do away with what was a wide area of the county's one and only livery stable.

Two days before the election, Jocelyn dropped into Noack's store to visit with Elsa and buy a few needs. Elsa shuffled back and forth behind the counter, rubbing her hands together. "I feel terrible, Jocelyn, giving up my council seat, being one of only two women on the board. The worst of it allows J.L. an opportunity to have my place, now that he's got himself on the ballot. I have to give it up, you know?" Her wrinkled brow deepened. "Regular meetings, emergency meetings, town folks' complaints, run a body ragged. I'm ready to do other things in what time I have from the store." She stopped pacing, added Jocelyn's purchases to her bill, then continued. "Our dear Mr. J.L. Cochran wants to be my replacement in the worst way, so that he can push hard his own agenda, get rid of your livery stable business, and bring in motorcars. I hope to heaven that he'll lose greatly against George Jacobsen."

"I know too well what Cochran is after, lately some nights it's hard to sleep. But I'm convinced that George, a fellow with a great deal more common sense than J.L. has, will win your seat on the council. Being a longtime, well-respected member of the business community with his feed store, knowing folks as well as he does, George deserves the position over a greedy, power-hungry newcomer like J.L. Cochran."

She'd voiced that opinion over and over in her conversations with friends, neighbors, and fellow-business owners in Skiddy as well as outside town. To anyone who would listen, actually. Occasionally the person had no interest whatsoever in the election, didn't care one way or the other who won. Others admitted they'd already accepted money, or favors to come, from Cochran, by agreeing to vote for him. Others were so convinced that J. L.'s plan was so foolhardy, nobody would vote for him and they needn't lose time from their work to vote, such an idiot would lose with or without them.

"J.L. Cochran has to lose," Elsa Noack was saying now, "or the greater loss will be to the town and its residents, not to mention outlying folks who need your livery as much as they need the sun to come up in the morning."

"Besides my battle with J.L. over my livery stable, I'm doing my best to mind other measures on the ballot, Elsa." Jocelyn moved around the store, choosing further items she needed at home, molasses, vanilla extract, coffee. She carried them to the counter and said lightly, "Such as the council wanting to use city funds to dig a well in the center of town and put in a fountain and resting benches. I like that, it would be nice, though not something absolutely necessary. We're Skiddy, Kansas, not Paris, France."

"You probably heard about the proposal to hire a new deputy to replace Deputy Cora, the marshal's wife?" Elsa stood behind the counter with her hands on her hips, smiling. "As y'all know, it was the councils' and the marshal's idea, not Cora's by any means, to take her deputy's badge. I don't think they'll budge her at all from being deputy."

Jocelyn laughed softly. "I agree. Cora loves her job as deputy, enjoys time away from keeping house and her four rambunctious children. Lucky for her that the two oldest are able to take her place at home, caring for the younger ones." She continued, thoughtful. "I'm neither here nor there about the measure suggesting new paint on the town hall, but I will probably vote for it, if money's available. And I agree that folks living in the city limits really need to keep their chickens and pigs well-penned. Or," she gave a teasing laugh, "hire somebody to herd them."

Mr. Noack, a slender man with a dark, full moustache turned and looked down from where he stocked a high shelf further away down the aisle of the store. "I wish you luck, Mrs. Pladson, for your concern about the ballot. J.L. has spent a fortune glad-handing and treating folks to large suppers at the hotel in his attempts to convince them to vote for him." He climbed down and walked over, brushing his hands together, saying to both women, "There isn't an inch of plank walk that he hasn't pounded up and down, talking to people about the matter, days on end. Hotel to the feed store, saloon to our store, bank to newspaper office." He rubbed his nose. "We may have to put a need for new plank walks on the ballot, if Cochran keeps on marching and bleating, wearing them out."

Mrs. Noack added, "And on Sundays, at church it's the same thing."

Her husband took time to slice and wrap cheese for a new customer, Elsa then taking over at the cash register.

Jocelyn attempted a sense of calm and ease as their conversation picked up again. "I'm so glad that women have the right to vote these days. I've shared some straight, honest conversations with many, making rounds to their homes. Next to none of the women go along with J.L. Cochran and his views. In fact, I ran into more tar-and-feather dislike of him than anything else, for his greed, cheating, and wild ideas."

Mr. Noack frowned. "Troubles me more'n a little, what I hear about Cochran paying a lot of folks to vote for him. Hard to believe that so many of them are plumb tickled at a money-deal with the scoundrel, in trade for their vote when day after tomorrow comes. It's plumb frightening how many folks put money before kindness, human need, before anything. I fear that the election can go either way, we won't know which that is 'til it's over."

"You're right of course, but as owner of the livery, and for the sake of so many others who need it, I hope Mr. Cochran loses. By a landslide." *But how could that be the result, with him buying so many promised votes for himself?* Mr. Noack was right, only time would tell. Unfortunately.

～

Jocelyn felt relief putting the coming election hullabaloo behind her for the time being and having a few moments alone at home with Rom, the two of them seated on a log down by the creek. He told her about his meeting with his father in Skiddy. "We meet and talk quite a bit, but nobody knows he's my pa. Folks just take him as a friendly newcomer who likes people and that ain't hard for him to do anymore. From bein' a salesman, I suppose."

"He's asked you to leave Skiddy with him, let him be a father to you again?" She watched his face closely, knowing that the two of them should possibly be together, but also not wanting him to leave if it wasn't something he truly wanted.

"He talked about that, right away, but I told him that I wanted to stay here, where I have a job and like livin' with you folks." His eyes met hers. "To tell the truth, I don't think he was much disappointed. He'd be on the road sellin' and I'd just be in the way taggin' along. Listenin' to his stories has been fun, we talked a bit about Nebraska and Weepin' Water, the town where we used to live—" His voice deepened with feeling. "We talked about my mother, how she died, how for so long we've missed her. I told him you are so much like a real Ma to me, it's hard to tell the difference."

"Thank you for that, Rom." She smiled at him, her heart singing, and gave his jaw a pat. "And you have to know that I love you like you are my born son, and I always will."

He grinned at her. "I know."

"Everything is keen between you and your father, then?"

He lifted a shoulder. "I dunno. Yeah, I reckon it is. If I ever need anything, he says to let him know." A flush crept up his neck and into his face and he looked off to the side. "He's so googly-eyed about that woman who was stayin' at your house, Nila's mother, and her the same about him, don't seem like much else is important."

"Googly-eyed, hmm?" Her spirits danced.

"That's for sure. I think if I had to be around the two of them much, I'd be sick."

"No, you wouldn't." She laughed and squeezed his arm. "Think how happy they make each other at their age? That's a good thing, whether for a short while or— or maybe the rest of their lives. A good thing."

He shook his head. "If you think so. It's no concern to me so it don't matter one way or the other." He scratched his jaw, and grinned. "I do like the new Pa as much as the old one, maybe even better."

"And Flaudie?"

"I thought it best to keep a hitch on my lip." He lifted his hat and then clapped it on again. "An' it ain't me that's googly-eyed."

She laughed. "Ah, Son, you have a lot to learn, but you have plenty of time and I do know that you're smarter by the day. You make me proud. I just want you to know here and now that you're one of the best things to happen to the Pladson family. Please, don't ever forget that, whatever you do, wherever you are."

The of them stood up, their talk over, Andy's voice squeaked behind them. Rom loped up the rise, grabbed Andy, and slung him over his shoulder like a bag of grain and led the way.

Watching them go, she wished that other matters in her life were half as enjoyable. Certainly, facing possible results of tomorrow's election was not one of them.

NINETEEN

Jocelyn sat high in their wagon beside Pete as they drove into town. Her worry over possible election results this day were partially lifted seeing groups of men and women already waiting on the walk outside Skiddy's town hall. Many others were walking in that direction. Dimming her excitement and hopes was J. L. Cochran's beetle-black Oldsmobile parked directly in front of the building, and Maretta Rudd's red Ford arriving at the moment, putting and trembling to a stop right behind the Oldsmobile.

"*The rich man's toy,* some call motorcars, I read in the newspaper the other day." Pete drew the team to a slow walk. "The horseless carriage, otherwise the motorcar, is 'a banner to prove how well off the motorist is and be admired for it'." He chuckled and scrubbed a hand down his face. "I suppose that's true, if they say so."

"It's hoity-toity hooey, is what it is. For pity's sake, they can't walk two blocks from their business, or their hotel to get here? They must park their blamed motorcars right in front of the town hall?" She cleared her throat. "Some days those two are more than I can take."

Pete patted her knee as they drew to a halt behind the livery stable. "Let's hope brains win over show-off fools today."

"I surely hope so. And should J.L. win from boughten votes, that will have to be looked into—I'd be most pleased if he's arrested for it and given a long sentence in jail." She took Pete's hand and climbed from the wagon. "Sorry I rattle on so, but the man gets my goat, and then some."

"Jail might teach him a thing or two," Pete agreed with a grin.

Arm in arm they headed for the town hall, following the crowd. As they walked by the two fancy motor cars parked in front, Jocelyn remembered something from her many conversations with folks about the upcoming election. "George Jacobsen said to me the other day that 'Skiddy and Morris County couldn't be a better place to live, what it *isn't* is a place of empty-headed show-offs who've got more money than they know what to do with'. Except, from what I hear concerning the money part, that probably isn't true about J.L. Cochran being rich 'more money than what he knows what to do with.'"

"Nope. The man is a sneaky crook, a pretender in the money department, according to Marshal Hillis. Like it's a game, he plays with money, loses it gambling, always borrowing, or using money to buy what he can't earn legitimately."

Jocelyn took a deep breath. "George just has to win the council seat. He'll help see that my livery stays." Her stomach churned knowing that there was an equal chance of it not happening—Cochran was as fixated as a bottled bumblebee. The churning inside her worsened as she looked up to see J.L. bustling toward them on the way out of the town hall.

Wearing a grin the size of a horse trough, he tipped his hat. "H'lo, there. Hope you folks are ready for a great change. It's about to happen, and say," he caught Pete's arm, his attitude genial, "we're all going to be the better for it, don't you know?" He looked bursting to say more, to convince them of it but Pete yanked his arm away and pushed by him, sheltering Jocelyn as they went.

"Good grief." Jocelyn glanced over shoulder. "He thinks he's already won, before the voting is over and votes are counted."

"He ought to hobble his lip, at least once in a while. Because you're a sweet lady, my good wife, I won't say what I think of that dirty rotten stinkin' cheatin' son-of-biscuit."

"Shush." She gave Pete a playful grin. Filled all at once with feelings of calm and ease, her head came up as they moved toward the voting table. "Even if he does win the councilman job, he can't get rid of my business, Pete. I'll fight like the devil on that until Cochran finally realizes it simply won't happen." *One way or another, I'll put him in his place once and for all.*

~

Two mornings later, Jocelyn was surprised to see Rom's father waiting outside the livery when she arrived. She drove her team and wagon around to the back and he strolled alongside, smiling as he offered his hand as she climbed from the wagon. "Good morning, uh—Mr. Clark, mmm—David. What brings you to the livery?" *You're not here to rent a horse and buggy, you have your own.* "Something about Rom? I still can't afford your set of silverware, if that's it."

His grin widened. "Just bringing good news that you might've not heard yet. There's been a lot of talk at the hotel that J. L. Cochran means to put you out of business. Start a motorcar sales business for himself in your location? As a councilman, he'd get the whole council to do away with your livery on account of it being a smelly nuisance? Something like that."

Over my dead body. "A lot like that."

"You might like to know, then, Mrs. Pladson, that Mr. Cochran lost the councilman seat to the other fella, by twenty-six votes. Heard the news just an hour ago." He thumbed his hat back. "It took the vote counters this long, two days, to finish the count, Mr. Cochran insisting on recounts over and over."

"He lost? The cockroach lost? Oh, my, that's the best news I'd ever hope to hear."

David Clark's eyes widened and he laughed. "Cockroach?"

Her face warmed in embarrassment. "Just a little nickname a friend gave him. I should have better manners, and not use it. From now on, I won't." She felt light hearted, like all her burdens had floated away. She stepped more lightly, almost skipping. "Mr. Cochran lost and George Jacobsen won. Thank Hannah."

Prank hustled forward to take care of her mule team. "Mornin' Missus. Howdy, Mr. Clark. You're lookin' mighty pert, Missus. You heard the news I reckon?"

"I'm feeling pert most definitely. And yes, Mr. Clark, here, just gave me wonderful news about the election that George Jacobsen won."

"Heard it myself just a while ago. The cockroach was plumb squashed, way I heard it." He laughed at his own joke and proceeded to unhitch Alice and Zenith. Freed, Alice waggled her tall ears and Zenith brayed, both no doubt anxious for the rest, feed and water.

David Clark had stood by, waiting. Clearly, he had something more on his mind than the election. About Rom, maybe, although she'd understood that had been settled. "Let's talk in the office, uh—David."

She pulled her chair away from her desk and motioned at the other for him. "What is it, Mr. Clark? You seem to have something to tell me? You're not leaving Skiddy yet, are you?"

He remained standing, his hands on the back of the chair. "Not just yet, but I will be leaving before long. I have other news and want you to know." He looked shy, but happy. "I've asked Mrs. Malone to be my wife."

Flaudie! At Jocelyn's intake of breath, her widened eyes, he hurried on.

"I know that may shock a few folks, Flaudie and I have known one another for a very short time. You see, I've been lonely more than I can describe, ever since I lost my first wife, back in Nebraska. Met a few other women here and yon since, but none of that ever worked out." His expression asked for backup. "Flaudie needs someone to take care of her. We get along together something special and decided we might as well get married. You understand, don't you, Jocelyn?"

Truth to tell, my mind is going crazy. "Of course, I do. That's wonderful news!" She stood to grab his hands in hers. "I'm very happy for both of you." *And relieved beyond any measurement imaginable.* She smiled at him and sat down again, chin in hand, looking at him in wonderment.

"I wanted you to know, because my son wants to continue living with your family." This time he sat in the chair and leaned forward. "Which I've agreed to, and he's told me that you're much in favor of him staying on. It is certainly more than agreeable with him. I'd like for us to always be in touch, though, always. Anything he needs, I want to know."

"Surely, whatever you say." Her heart settled to a reasonable beat.

"Flaudie and I will be traveling. As soon as the Justice of the Peace officially makes us man and wife, we're heading down south. Flaudie's always wanted to see the grand plantations down there, and it will be a fine part of the country for me to ply my trade."

"My genuine congratulations to you both. Sweet Hannah, but if this isn't the best day I've had—well starting to have, in a long time."

'I'm glad I helped make it so." He reached for her hand and his lips brushed her fingers, his smile warm. "You're a wonderful woman, Mrs. Pladson. Your husband, Pete, is very lucky."

Of all things! That shabby farmer from Nebraska had assuredly changed. And marrying Flaudie Malone? Strangely, this marrying seemed right. Who would have ever guessed?

The following week passed in glorious calm for Jocelyn. Whenever they crossed paths, J. L. Cochran was stony faced and stone deaf to her attempt at a greeting, as though she didn't exist. Then came the day she drove into town, surprised to see that Maretta's Hat Shop was being emptied, trunks and hat boxes piled outside on the plank walk. Jocelyn continued to the livery, turned her rig over to Prank, and hurried back to the hat shop. A well-dressed man, a stranger to Jocelyn, talked to a railroad station helper who was loading Maretta's things onto a wagon while a group of locals watched. The gentleman then assisted a stormy-faced Maretta to the passenger side of her red Ford motorcar. She yanked her arm from his hand and climbed in. Not seeming the least aggrieved at her behavior, he cranked the machine until it rumbled to life, went around to the driver side and climbed in. The motorcar coughed and chugged down the street.

Jocelyn went over to Elise, Nila's friend who worked part time for Maretta in the hat shop. "What in the name of Hannah is going on, Elise? Was that man taking her by force? Who is he, do you know? I see everything emptied and..."

Elise's smile wavered. "I'm not supposed to say the truth. But now that she's going, I can't see what'd hurt. Instead of the facts, Maretta insisted that I tell people she had to close up the shop because of you and your livery. Said that I was to be sure to say that she couldn't tolerate the 'horsey stink and other smells' of the livery another day, they were making her deathly ill. And she had no choice."

"Putting all the blame on me, and my business with

horses and mules? Ah, well," she half-smiled and shook her head. "I'm not too surprised at that, but there are other reasons, besides? I hope."

"Yes, Mrs. Pladson, I don't want to lie and you might as well know the truth. Maretta broke down and sobbing her heart out, told me quite a bit what was happening to her recently." She hesitated a second. "Maretta was being investigated by the Skiddy marshal through the law back where she came from, looking into her background and all." She scratched her arm, bit her lip.

"There's nothing wrong with you telling me this, Elise." She reached to touch her arm, comforting her nerves. "I'd already heard a bit about that a short time ago. I wasn't sure how serious it was, though. Why would she be investigated? Had she committed a crime —surely must've been for something?"

"It all came about at the request of an Iowa man who claimed she robbed him." She motioned with her head. "That's him you saw, taking her and her motorcar. I overheard more, when that particular fella came here to Skiddy and her shop some days back. Seems that Maretta had left her husband, his name, Calvin Rudd, part of a rich, but miserly family, to take up with one of his wealthy friends, Upton Hewitt. That's the name of the fella who came looking for her, the one you saw."

"My heavens."

"Yeah. Time came when she and Mr. Hewitt began to argue over every little thing, according to him. I heard her admit that she'd figured out that her time with him and his money was over. It seems that while he was sleeping, soused with drink, she emptied his pockets, slipped off his valuable solid gold and sapphire ring and cufflinks, grabbed a few other valuables, and ran, planning to never be found." She hesitated a moment. "His own investigating proved that she bought the red Model A Ford with his ring."

Jocelyn clapped a hand over her mouth, shaking her head in shock. "If that don't beat all. The same motorcar that then brought her here to Skiddy—to make a new life with J. L. Cochran and have a motorcar business. A try at that, anyway."

"Yes, well it's over. Upton Hewitt finally found her, and two days ago showed up to square things with Maretta. I don't know all the details that went on between Mr. Hewitt and the law but I understand that when the marshal offered to arrest Maretta for what she'd done, Mr. Hewitt didn't want that. He did insist on having the motorcar and the rest of his stuff that she stole. Kind of a nice fella, seemed to me. He agreed to take her back to Des Moines, Iowa, and turn her over to her family, corn and pig farmers near Des Moines."

Jocelyn rubbed her forehead. "Pig farmers. And Maretta thought my livery smelled bad?"

"Mostly she was wanting to side in with J.L. in a fancy new moneymaking business, motorcars, like you said. But she maybe didn't like the smell of the farm she grew up on, either. If she hadn't been so greedy on top of stealing, she might not've had to land right back where she came from."

Her shop was now empty—Jocelyn couldn't help feeling a bit sad, turning to look at it. She might've owed Maretta an apology for parking her motorcar in front of the town hall election day, not walking there. Maybe that'd been for a quick get-away if needed.

"Thanks, Elise. If Maretta wants it believed that she

had to leave town because of my livery stable, I really don't mind. I do wish that we could've somehow been friends. Maretta was talented, the hats she made were beautiful."

If she and Mr. Hewitt had taken J.R. with them, the situation would have turned out perfectly. Unfortunately, that didn't happen.

~

J. L. was still seen around town, somewhat edgy tending to his affairs as a businessman fairly recent to Skiddy. According to rumors, and suggestions by Deputy Cora Hillis and the marshal, he was deep in trouble with the local bank. Maintaining his old habit of taking out a mortgage to buy a business, in the process borrowing more than needed. When the note was called in, which it was often about to, his usual trick was to skip town, take with him the borrowed funds to invest in another business or two in yet another town.

He survived on borrowed money, leaving a trail of unlawful debt that included banks, country loan brokers, city loan sharks, and private citizens who had money to loan and would now like to wring his neck with a hanging rope. It was his habit to always use the excess money for himself. The bank, or another situation making the loan, took back the business he walked away from. Which he considered fair, but banks and the law saw his shenanigans quite differently.

Jocelyn was thinking about Cochran's troubles as she drove toward Skiddy, lines in hand, tapping her mules with them every so often. Anyone could see that J.L. 's debt problems were his own doing, considering his 'easy come, easy go' big spender way of life. She was so glad she'd paid off the loans that it had taken to buy her livery business.

As she neared town, she began to have an eerie, off-guard feeling which worsened in spades as she drove along main street and saw the churn of people at the open doors of her livery, looking inside. *What in the name of Hannah was going on now?* A cluster of friends from town rushed grim-faced to meet her as she climbed from the wagon, all talking at once.

"Your stable's been hit bad, Missus."

"Bashed up inside with pickaxes and crowbars so much you wouldn't know where you was."

"Gates are all left open. Your animals gone."

"'Ceptin' a mule or two grazin' on down the street."

"Blood spatters on the wall where the office was. Other places," a man growled in pity.

Feeling like screaming, her breath catching, she asked, pushing through the crowd, "Rom, where is he? Where is Prank?" Heart pounding, fists doubled, she tripped and struggled a path through debris of smashed stalls, bashed feeders, hacked troughs.

Someone caught her elbow, stopped her. It was her friend from the feed store, George Jacobsen.

"They ain't here, Mrs. Pladson. They're at Dr. Asherwood's, he has 'em at his hospital."

"Oh, dear god, no! The hospital." She broke into a run down the street, pushing people aside that wanted to help her, and ran faster.

TWENTY

"Rom. Prank. Please be all right, please." Jocelyn hurriedly swiped at tears as she ran toward the little hospital, her scrambled thoughts trying to understand. *Who would do this to them and why? J. L. Cochran, was who, but he couldn't have done all that damage to the livery, not by himself and sent Rom and Prank to the hospital with injuries, too. He had to've had help, a gang, the trashing done quick, and at night, before someone else heard, or witnessed what they were doing and stopped them. And Rom and Prank, suffering from beatings? How badly? Would they recover?*

Whoever did all this, they deserved jail, no, hanging.

Deputy Cora Hillis grabbed her as she burst through the door of the hospital. "Here now, slow down," she said gently, holding Jocelyn tight.

"I have to see them. How are they? They aren't...?" Chills raced up and down her spine, a lump as big as an egg choked her throat and tears filled her eyes.

"You can't see them now. Doc is patching them up. Don't cry, hon."

Jocelyn grabbed her arms. "Please, Cora, tell me what happened to them?"

She took so long, her eyes sympathetic, Jocelyn thought she'd never speak although it was just seconds. "Both the old man and boy were beat up bad with clubs of some kind, axe handles maybe, but they are alive and they'll heal in time. Prank is hurt a little the worse, beat like he was at his age, it's a wonder that he's alive. Come sit over here, sweetheart," she caught Jocelyn's elbow and led her to the waiting room's sofa. "Doc will be finished pretty soon, you'll get to see them."

"I don't understand." Jocelyn wiped her eyes, struggled to be calm and halt the chattering of her teeth. "Those two did nothing w-wrong. My l-livery wasn't hurting anything, not really. H-have you, or has the marshal found out who did this? Whoever it was, were they c-caught?" Her fists tightened, her nails cutting into her palms.

"Marshal's on their tail right now, with several men in his posse, to help. Your boy was able to talk, a little. He said three men did it, axed and ripped the livery, the stalls, bins, everything, to pieces. Took the money from the office. He and Prank fought their best to stop them, but three outlaw scums against a young fella and an old man—they got the best of them."

An angry sob caught in Jocelyn's throat. She motioned with a shaking hand for Cora to continue.

"The outlaws wanted to steal the horses for themselves, were in a hurry to get away before they was heard, or seen, and found out. While they gathered up the horses from their stalls, Rom crawled out of sight, pulling Prank with him into a storage bin. Covered the both of them with empty feed sacks. If he hadn't a done that they'd likely have been finished with a bullet, killed so they wouldn't talk. You be glad, woman, that the two of them escaped the worst."

A rush of relief filled her and she was finally able to breathe. "I am glad. So much." She clutched a cameo at her throat for comfort. "J. L. Cochran is behind this. I know it in my soul. If he couldn't get rid of my business any other way, he'd hire it destroyed. And he'd not mind if anyone who got in the way was hurt. Killed, even." She rubbed the goosebumps from her arms. "No doubt he ordered it done, giving him someone else to blame. He's been that desperate."

"He's behind what's been done for certain."

"You know something then?" Jocelyn shivered and clutched her folded arms to her body.

"Yes. The hotel manager called us in the middle of the night, told the marshal a gunshot had just been heard there, inside the hotel." She looked grim. "My husband found Cochran bleeding in his room, trying again to kill himself, his first shot to the head just grazed his skull."

"What?" Jocelyn stared wide-eyed at her, for a few seconds turned to stone from shock. "Where is J.L. now, what happened, did Marshal Hillis get a confession out of him that he did this? And who helped him?" She swallowed hard, wanting to know every last thing, especially who was mixed in with J.L. and the damage they'd done.

"Cochran is in jail. Nursing a very bad headache." She grinned maliciously. "Marshal said he was babbling like a baby when he found him. Admitted he tried to commit suicide and failed, wanted to keep trying. Marshal took the gun away from him, made out to sympathize, told J.L. that he'd be fine, that there was no good reason to kill himself. Cochran broke down and told him who his accomplices were, everything. It was some renegades who were available for hire. He hardly knew them."

"Did he try to kill himself because of me, then? The fact that I wouldn't let him have his way about the livery and simmering because he lost the election, too? I don't understand. He surely wouldn't try to commit suicide because his outlaw bunch destroyed the livery like they did. He'd be so happy about that he'd likely break his arm patting himself on the back. Wiping me out was his reason to hire them in the first place."

"Jocelyn, dear woman, don't think you're to blame for any of this, especially his attempt to kill himself. It ain't all that, it's mostly the money troubles he's got himself into. He wasn't more than a day or two away from being jailed and taken to trial for all the debt he's made and not paid. Think about that. From the information Leo and I learned, he's left a trail of huge unpaid debt everywhere he's been, but has been too wily to be caught and held responsible. Until now." She grinned. "Now we got lucky."

"I'd heard about the bad debts. And I'm mighty glad he's in jail."

Cora wore a knowing smile, hands at her waist, elbows wide. "Constant playacting that you're rich, a millionaire even, can be pretty costly. An' that's what Mr. Cochran has finally learned. It's pretty definite that he hired the outlaws to get revenge against you as well as removing the livery out of his way. Too late, the poor fool surely realized that even if he ran, he'd be caught. Go to jail for having your boy and the old man, Prank, nearly beat to death. Likely worried that one or the other might die from the beating, and that would be a charge of murder. Not to mention the trouble he was in for all the debts he owed in Kansas an' Iowa, an' who all knows where else." There was a tightness in her expression, her lips flattened. "He knew damned well he'd be hung for it all, an' he tried to take the easy way out. The easy way. Only the fool missed an' only injured himself a trifle."

Jocelyn looked at her, thinking. *My fault, at least partly because I stood up to him and he was never going to get rid of my livery, at least not in a legal way. But wanting to have my own business is no call to nearly kill two people I dearly love, and trash my livery near to nothing. Then steal my horses and mules, take the livery's hard-earned money.* "Who provided the pick-axes and what all to trash my livery, if they were men on horseback, they couldn't carry all that with them, could they?"

"Not easy." She leaned forward, hands clasped in her lap. "Which takes us back to J.L. Cochran. It was him. He did it. Borrowed a wagon and team that belonged to another hotel guest, was seen leaving in it well after dark. After the marshal found Cochran bleeding and took him to jail, he found the wagon behind the hotel, brand new pickaxes, crowbars and such in it—probably borrowed from Cochran's own hardware store."

Jocelyn was speechless. Wishing with all her soul that none of this nightmare was true.

Cora gave her a pat. "I need to get back to Leo's office and see if our prisoner needs anything." She scoffed at that, then grew serious. "You set here and don't worry. Everything is going to be fine, hon. It'll take a little time, is all. Just hang on."

"Thank you, Cora." She grasped her hands. "I feel better just knowing that J.L. Cochran will get his due."

～

It seemed an eternity passed before Doctor Asherwood came to the hospital's front room where Jocelyn waited. "Sorry I kept you waiting, Mrs. Pladson."

She sprang to her feet. "I understand, doctor. How are they? They're ali—alive, both of them?"

"Yes, they are in bad shape, but alive." He stood with hands shoved into the pockets of his white coat, his expression serious. "Prank Morgan will live, but it's questionable if he'll still have sight in his left eye, he was struck hard there with something."

"No!" Her hands clenched.

"Sorry to have to tell you, Jocelyn," he said gently, "but yes, the hoodlums showed no mercy. Mr. Morgan's cracked ribs and some cuts on his arms will heal in time, the bruises—pretty much all over his body—will fade along with the pain. Your son has a broken leg, which I've set and at his age, when healed it should be as good as new. He had a dislocated shoulder which I put back in place. Same as the old fellow, he has a cracked rib or two, bruises, swelling, cuts."

Jocelyn listened, her hand to her mouth, tears clouding her eyes. *How could they do this to two sweet people? So damnably unfair!*

Doctor Asherwood continued. "The young man was able to talk a bit when they brought him in. He'd been sleeping in the loft, he said. Prank sleeping on the cot he has down in part of the office. They beat on Prank first. Your boy heard them, scrambled down the loft ladder and went after them, tried every way to stop them from beating the old fellow. Did the best he could, and it could have been worse if he hadn't come to the old man's defense."

"Can I see them, please?" She swiped at her eyes, straightened her back.

"Sorry again." His tone gentled further. "Neither is awake just now, I had to give them laudanum to prevent as much pain and distress as possible cleaning and taking care of their cuts and fractures." He rocked back on his heels, smiling encouragement. "Have heart, Mrs. Pladson. They have a lot of healing to do, both of them, but bullets would have been worse. We might have lost them. Let's remember that, and be glad."

"They'll get well then?" At his nod she heaved a sigh of relief.

"I'm certain of it. The old fella may take longer to heal, due to his age. The young man will be good as new in a few weeks. Why don't you come back later, when they'll be awake?"

"I want to see them now. Please." *I have to see for myself that they are breathing. It doesn't matter that they are asleep.*

He hesitated a moment, sighed, then motioned her to follow.

She wiped her eyes, brushed her hair back from her face, straightened her shoulders, and entered the room.

Swallowing back the lump in her throat, she bent and laid her cheek against Rom's quiet swollen face—and left it there for a tick of several heart-breaking seconds. At the second bed, she lay her hand lightly against Prank's jaw, below the eye bandage. She took a chair near their beds and looked up at Doctor Ashwood. "These two have been so good to me, both good, decent souls that don't deserve this." She wiped her eyes on the back of her hand. "I'd like to sit for a while, if you don't mind?"

He kindly gave in. "Of course. As long as you want, Mrs. Pladson. May I treat you to a cup of tea? I'm needing one myself."

"If it's no bother, yes, please." It was going to take more than tea, though, to wash the pain in her heart away.

❧

Early the next morning, Jocelyn and Pete scrambled to complete their chores, anxious to return to Skiddy and check on Prank and Rom. The near demolished livery stable was also on their list. Nila stood on the porch, Andy's hand in hers, as they were leaving. "Tell Rom that me and Andy love him, and that we want him to get well soon. Mr. Morgan—Prank, let him know, too, that we're thinking of him and wish for him to get better right away." Andy clung tight to Nila's hand and echoed, "Tell 'em."

Jocelyn smiled. "We will. And you two take care here at home. We'll be back as soon as we can."

"Bye Momma, bye Pa." Andy waved furiously, moving forward a couple steps, slight worry on his face.

"Be good for Nila, Son. We won't be gone long." She blew him a kiss. *If only it were possible to be everywhere at once. Someday she was going to have that problem worked out to a fare thee well, God willing*

At the hospital, Prank was still asleep but breathing soundly and steady. Rom was awake, but groggy. Jocelyn did everything she could to hide her reaction to the swelling, the bruises, and patched cuts on their faces.

"How are you, Son? I'm so sorry this happened to you and Prank."

He struggled to speak, "Ain—ain't your f-fault, Ma. W-was th-them b-buggers ol' J-J. L. s-sent to d-do us in."

"I know, Son, I know. But I'm still deeply sorry. Neither you nor Prank deserved to be beat on like this."

Pete stepped closer to the bed. "We're damn proud of you, Rom, for throwing yourself into the fray like you did to help Prank. An' makin' sure you both were safe from those scoundrels' further intentions to harm you."

"Th-they w-were busy wr-wreckin' ever-everything. G-getting' r-ready t-to take the h-horses, st-steal th-them, I-I heard th-em talk-talking' of ki-killin' us n-next. I h-hid us aw-away."

Jocelyn held his hand, her eyes smarting. "You did a wonderful thing, Rom, you saved both your lives. You'll be commended for that as long as you live. We couldn't be happier that you both are going to be just fine."

"I-I want to go h-home."

She was silent for a moment. "And we'd like to take you home, Rom. But Doctor Ashwood wants to keep you here in his hospital a few more days, your more serious injuries under his care yet a while." When he looked like he might complain, she said, "Nila is making cherry hand pies for you, we'll bring some our next visit.

If you're able to eat such?" She stroked her face, patted her jaws, indicating her meaning.

"I—I'll b-be ab-able." His eyes flashed ironclad certainty. Bringing Pete's chuckle.

"That's my boy."

They sat with him a while longer, waiting for Prank in the next bed to wake. He still slept soundly and they could only be glad for that, how it'd help his older bones heal.

Rom's eyes began to repeatedly close and he was soon asleep as well.

Pete caught her hand and pulled Jocelyn to her feet. "Need to get over to the livery, Jocey, and the mess there," he whispered.

She cleared her throat and fell in step with him, dread at thought of the demolished livery, a roil rising in her stomach.

TWENTY-ONE

J ocelyn's breath caught when she and Pete neared the livery site. Like busy bees, clusters of friends and town-folk were at work cleaning up the wreckage. *They hadn't needed to do that.* When she and Pete had driven by earlier, her business place was just an ugly abandoned catastrophe. *In time, I'll know just what I want to do, but this...*

The moment they left the wagon they were surrounded. Swamped with exclamations meant to lift their spirits, and question after question. As best they could, they explained to the crowd what they knew about J.L. Cochran's part in the crime. That he was in jail. Had tried to commit suicide evidently to avoid jail, or a hanging. In conversations about the cruel beatings given Prank and Rom, murmurings of sympathy began all over again along with ripe swearing at the ones who'd been so cruel.

"Look there, hon." Pete came and drew her out of a circle of women-friends. She looked where he pointed, clasped her palms together and gave a happy squeal, her heart racing. Marshal Hillis rode in the lead, and right behind him, surrounded by the posse, were three sullen hardcases, hands tied behind them, slumped on their horses. Jocelyn noted immediately that they'd been dealt some of the same treatment they'd given Rom and Prank. *Fine*.

Close behind, further members of the posse herded the livery's missing horses and mules. Clapping and loud cheers rose to an ear splitting chorus, drowning out Jocelyn's "They have them! The ones who did this. My animals, too, my horses and mules. Thank Hannah."

Pete put his arm around her. He leaned over to kiss her cheek. "This is just a damned good day, isn't it sweetheart?" He moved away then, and motioned to the group herding the stolen animals. "Put them in the corrals out back, about the only thing these worthless human beings didn't ruin. The horses and mules, that is, put them in the corral." He growled toward the outlaws, "Them bushwhacking devils can go straight to jail, or hell." Smiling, he led the way to the corrals, opening gates for the blowing, head-tossing herd, closing the gates after they'd trotted past him to the water and feed troughs and deep, waving grass.

~

For the next week, Jocelyn spent a major part of her time in Skiddy visiting Rom and Prank at the hospital, more often than not refusing to look in the direction of the miserable shambles of her livery as she passed by. Such as today, wagon wheels creaking as she headed on toward the hospital. She was still thinking what she might do about the livery property, *ought she to rebuild, or would she rather not?* In time, she felt that she'd have a sure plan. She simply wasn't ready and there were more important things for her attention. Like now—her mood climbed in excitement—Rom was being released from the hospital today and would be coming home to Nickel Hill.

Doctor Ashwood handed Rom his crutches. "You be sure to use these, Rom. If you try getting around without them too soon, you'll end up right back here in the hospital and maybe surgery."

"Sure, Doc, I intend to use them 'til my leg's healed. I might be cussin' those hooligans that did this to me, now and then, but otherwise I'll be doin' fine back on the ranch." His crutches clumping, he looked over his shoulder at Prank, sitting up in his bed now, pillows behind him. "I'll miss you, ol' man, so you hurry up and heal, too."

"I'm sorry you have to stay another week or two, Mr. Morgan—Prank," Doctor Ashwood said. "But you have more healing to do. I want to be sure you're fit to be up and around—right now you're not ready." The doctor turned to Jocelyn, "He's going to need a place to go, now that the livery is gutted, his spot in the livery office, gone."

"He does have a place to go, I'm taking him home to the ranch."

Prank leaned forward to protest, then groaned at the pain it caused him and sat back puffing. 'Missus, I ain't wantin' to burden you. I'll find somethin' my ownself."

"Heavens, Prank, you won't be a burden." She walked over and took his rough, gnarled hand in hers. "We want you there. You and Homer, both. When you're fully recovered, you're going to be a Nickel Hill hired hand. For pay."

Looking down, Jocelyn saw Prank's chest visibly expand some, his wrinkled old face—beat up as it was—bloomed with pride. "Well, shore." She could see that it hurt him to breathe. "We can help you out there on the ranch, I'm obliged to." His breath caught, "Won't—won't be no different than runnin' the livery for ya' I 'spect."

"A lot the same, some a little different but I know you'll do fine." She smiled at Rom, sitting on the edge of his bed, crutches in hand. "Are you ready, Son?"

He hopped up, grinning, and shoved the crutches in place. "Couldn't be readier."

~

I n no time, it seemed, Prank was able to come to Nickel Hill to live, too. His delight in moving into the bunkhouse, where Rom already had his own space and bed, couldn't be measured. Homer, on the other hand, had chosen to remain in his little house in Skiddy, handy to stores and such.

"Doctor Ashwood was right again," Jocelyn said one day when they were all sitting outside on quilts by the creek, following a small picnic. "When you were little, Rom, and first came to us, you were terribly sick with pneumonia. Doc had all the right information to get you well. That being mostly rest. Now, again, you're practically healed."

"Durn glad of it, had to heal or else. An' shoot, it's been long enough since those hooligans tried to kill us and destroyed the livery. I want all this behind me and forgotten when next summer comes, or the next, and I go back to Oklahoma and the 101 Ranch and the Real West Show."

"It'll happen, I don't have a doubt. And you, dear Prank," she faced him seated nearby, chomping on a chicken leg, "you're doing pretty fine yourself, on your way to healing up." It was taking time, he still hurt some when he moved, but talking came easier now. With each day here on the ranch, sitting on the porch, or at mealtime, telling his stories—most having to do with his part in the War Between the States—he was clearly getting better and itching to take on minor chores in the garden and at the barn.

"Near to killed us, those sidewinders. Would'a if the boy here hadn't drug me out of the way an' hid us. Yup, I'd be dead and Rom, mebbe, too." He automatically touched a crooked finger to the patch on his eye—getting used to having sight from only one eye hadn't come easy. Most of the time, he seemed rather proud of the black patch, bragged of looking 'like a pirate.' "I'm real sorry we couldn't stop them shysters from destroyin' your livery, Missus, they oughta been hung for that. Glad there ain't airy one of 'em got away with it, and the jury charged 'em with attempted murder, anyways, for what they did to the boy and me. Several years in prison won't be no picnic. Not for old Cockroach, neither, for puttin' them crooks onto us and for all his money cheatin'."

"No, the penitentiary won't be a picnic, and I'm glad of it. Those men were fools to follow J.L. Cochran's orders. Had they paid him no heed, they might've been free right now, even if he wasn't. That's if they didn't have more crimes in mind—and they probably did. Well, enough of that, it's over and done."

"'Cept for the livery, we all got to get that rebuilt."

Jocelyn looked at him, and smiled.

As the weeks passed, most of the rubble inside the destroyed livery site had been burned or removed but no effort had been taken so far to rebuild. Friends and neighbors by the dozen had offered to help build stalls and such but Jocelyn had asked them to wait a bit, she was in no hurry. One day, she and Pete were on the site, stacking what used lumber could be salvaged. Setting aside buckets, and other odds and ends. "Let's take a minute and talk," Pete said, arranging a couple of kegs for seats.

She sagged onto her keg, head in her hands, tired to the bone. "What?" She raised her head to look at him, brushed her hair back with dirty hands.

"Folks've been offering to help rebuild and you've been putting them off." He waved at the emptiness around them. Where stalls and horses, the sounds the animals made, feed and water troughs, stacks of hay, the office and more, used to be. "I need to know why. I thought you liked owning the livery, having your mule sales. We've got nothing but the outside of a livery barn left, and the hay barn outside, but we can do this, Jocey. It'll cost us plenty to fix the livery, but we'll figure it out."

"I've had thoughts about it, Pete, when I have even a minute to think. One I discounted, so didn't bother to mention it to you. I'm thinking now that it's a pretty good plan that I want us to take into consideration. You may like it, and then you might not."

"Well, shoot, go ahead. What is it, hon? I've been worried that you haven't been all fired up to rebuild right away. Not that you haven't had a lot to do with Rom and Prank, getting them well and settled in at home. Not to mention little Andy, growing fast and livelier every day." He rubbed his arm. "You ain't decided to quit the livery business, have you?" He chuckled in disbelief at his own remark.

"Not altogether, no, just some changes, which I've decided would be better all around. If you approve."

"What changes?" His long fingers cupped his chin and he frowned.

She looked him directly in the eye and let out a long breath. "George Jacobsen approached me the other day, when I was in Skiddy, to let me know that he'd like to have the livery located down by his feed store, if I wasn't going to rebuild where it's been."

Pete leaned back, eyes wide in surprise.

"I still wasn't sure what I wanted to do, so I didn't give him an answer. It bothered me, too, that my stubborn fighting back against J.L. and what he wanted, almost got Rom, and Prank, killed. Don't think I didn't love the business, mule trading, owning a livery stable, Pete. It was very important to me and still is. I agree that Skiddy has to have a livery and I'll support one to my last breath, but this time it may partly be somebody else's business."

"How so?" Worry wrinkled his brow.

Her lips pursed and she shrugged. "Like I said, George Jacobsen would like to have a livery on land he owns down by his feed store. It'd be further out of town and that would make some folks happy. I've talked to him again and we about have a deal, but that depends on how you feel concerning it. If we're not rebuilding, he wants anything left from the livery that's useful to help equip his stable, like the saddles and other tack that wasn't chopped up, the buggies that can be repaired. He'd pay us for that, and for the horses and mules the posse brought back. He'd need them for hitching to the buggies, and for riders who need to rent them."

"I'll be damned. Go ahead." He crossed his legs, found the post behind him with his shoulders and leaned back against it, hands behind his head.

"I'll still own the land here and the shell of the barn, the pastures and corrals. The big barn. For now, he'd pasture the horses and mules where they are, right here." Her voice began to lift with excitement. "I'd rent the hay barn to him and to other folks for horse and mule sales, this empty livery for whatever use it's needed for as part of that. I'd still be involved in the mule sales, partially."

"You've sure taken me by surprise, Jocey. But go ahead."

"I surprise myself, sometimes." She laughed softly. "But I'm pretty sure about this, Pete. I want to be home more, with our young'uns. Rom and Nila won't be with us much longer and I'd hate to miss a minute. Andy is growing and changing so much I don't want to miss that. Being a part-time businesswoman sounds perfect to me. I'd like to go ahead with it, if you like the idea, too."

He was quiet, looking at her with amusement, and

wonder. "I'd like to think about it, some. But it already sounds pretty good."

"That almost sounds like a yes to me." She waited.

He laughed at her. "All right, hell yes, darlin' it's a yes." He gave her a studied look, still chuckling. He slapped his knee. "How about we go on down to the feed store and tell George we agree with his offer. Work out the plans some more, if we have to. How about it?"

She looked down at herself, her hands, the filthy hems of her dress, couldn't imagine how dirty and messy her hair looked. "Give me a minute out at a trough by the windmill, and I'll be right back."

It took a little time and effort, but she decided when finished that she at least wasn't as dirty and sweaty as before. She felt cool, and comfortable from washing up in the hot afternoon. "I'm ready. I know that I still look terrible but it'll have to do."

"You look beautiful. If I had a mirror, right now, I could prove it."

"And you are something of a liar, but I purely love you anyway."

Arm in arm, they walked down the street to tell George they were ready for a partnership. "Are you sure of this, sweetheart, it's a risk you know." Pete lifted her hand and kissed it.

"What risk? Remember what you said when we talked about our first bank loan, to buy the livery?"

"Uh...I don't think so." He drew them to a stop.

'You said, 'this ain't the bottom, hon, it's the way up'."

He laughed and gave her a hug.

"There's more, Pete. Someday in the future, I think I'd like for us to have a nice motorcar business where the livery was. I'd sell Fords, maybe, but not Oldsmobiles, that'd remind me too much of J.L Cochran. Yes. Fords and maybe Cadillacs."

"What?" He shuffled back a step. "What are you sayin'? I can't believe this."

"I never said never, Pete, to motorcars. I said 'not yet' 'not for several years' and that's exactly what I meant."

He whirled her to face him and kissed her hard. They both laughed, looking to see if anyone had seen them kissing out on the street.

"We better hurry up if we're going to talk to George, or your plan will be nobody's business."

"It can wait, if you want to kiss me again." She turned to him, closed her eyes and stood on tiptoe.

He wanted.

A Look At: The Women of Paragon Springs
The Complete Series

THE DUST, THE WIND, THE PAIN

Award winning author Irene Bennet Brown introduces the four women of the thriving western Kansas town, Paragon Springs.

Cassiday Curran, Meg Brennon, Aurelia Symington and Lucy Walsh all found themselves in Paragon Springs in different ways, but they all have one thing in common: homesteading in a small western town while battling their own problems and the issues of life in the late 1800's.

Running from abusive husbands, falling in love, grief and ridicule are only some of the everyday struggles these women face. How they find their way through the struggles are what pull you into these heartwarming stories.

Women of Paragon Springs includes: Long Road Turning, Blue Horizons, No Other Place and Reap The South Wind.

"If you enjoy western novels, such as Little House on the Prairie and Lonesome Dove, you will enjoy this series by Irene Bennett Brown."

AVAILABLE NOW

ABOUT THE AUTHOR

Irene Bennett Brown is an award-winning author who enjoys using Kansas, where she was born, as background for her historical novels for both children and adults. She is a recipient of the Western Writers of America Owen Wister Award, and induction into Western Writers of America Hall of Fame. Other awards include Western Writers of America Spur Award, the Will Rogers Medallion Award, a nomination for the Mark Twain Award and other honors.

She lives with her husband, Bob, a retired research chemist, on two fruitful acres along the Santiam River in Oregon.

Irene Bennett Brown is an award-winning author who enjoys using Kansas where she was born, as backdrop for her historical novels for both children and adults. She is a recipient of the Western Writers of America Owen Wister Award and induction into Western Writers of America Hall of Fame. Other awards include Western Writers of America Spur Award, the Will Rogers Medallion Award, a nomination for the Mark Twain Award and other honors.

CPSIA information can be obtained
at www.ICGtesting.com
Printed in the USA
BVHW031649180723
667439BV00005B/61

9 781639 777822